HONEYMOON IN THE CARDS

A SUMMIT SPRINGS NOVEL

JODI PAYNE

BA TORTUGA

Honeymoon in the Cards

Cover illustration by AJ Corza
http://www.seeingstatic.com/
Cover content is for illustrative purposes only and any person depicted on the cover is a model.

ISBN: 978-1-951011-97-0

Published by Tygerseye Publishing, LLC
December 2023
Printed in the USA

As always, to our wives.
Merry Christmas!

1

Marissa listened to the phone ring, still not sure exactly what she was going to say when someone answered. It wasn't every day one had to cancel a honeymoon, especially not a free one.

She supposed that the lesson here was not to put the cart before the horse. After three years though, she'd thought it was reasonable to propose. She'd picked out a ring, made dinner reservations, she'd even hired a limo to take them to a hotel after Josie said yes.

But Josie didn't say yes.

How long was this phone going to ring? Shouldn't she have gone through to voicemail or something by now?

Finally, a chirpy voice answered. "Pines Peak Resort, how can I direct your call?"

"Oh. Well, I won a honeymoon package and I need to talk to—" She looked at the business card stapled to the folder full of brochures and information. "To Bryan Harker about it."

"Oh, of course. I'll get him for you. Just a sec!"

God, was anyone really that happy?

She wasn't.

Even the hold music was cheerful. How annoying was that?

She was just about ready to drop her cell phone down the garbage disposal when someone finally answered.

"Marketing."

"Bryan Harker, please?"

"Yep. Hang on."

Oh god. She was being put on hold again.

She was going to bite something. Hard. Hopefully hard enough her cheating bitch of an ex felt it.

"This is Bryan. Can I help you?"

"Yes. Hi, Bryan. This is Marissa Martin. I won a honeymoon package at your resort. We are supposed to come next weekend."

"Hello, Ms. Martin. Or I supposed it's Mrs. Martin by now? Congratulations. We're looking forward to rolling out the red carpet for you and your wife."

Fuck. She was going to throw up. Her cheeks heated and the knot in her stomach started doing somersaults. She needed to get off the phone. "I'm uh—unfortunately I—we —" She forced herself to take a breath.

Suck it up and get it over with Mari.

"We didn't get married. We're not coming. It's off. Everything is off."

"I—What?" That was utter shock. Just complete blankness, and if it didn't suck so hard, it would be funny as hell.

"Yeah. Sorry. Thanks for everything. Just send me a bill for...whatever you need to. It's fine. It's all fine." She sounded like an idiot, which, obviously, she was.

"Oh. Well, I'm sorry about all of that but...you have to come."

What? "Excuse me?"

"I mean...don't you still need a vacation? We'd love to have you. There might be a few...logistical matters, but I'm sure we can work something out."

Had this guy lost his mind?

"You heard me, right? I'm not taking a vacation with the bitch who didn't marry me. Excuse my French." Did she need to spell out how Josie had just flatly explained that she was in love with someone else? Mari wasn't going away with that bitch. She didn't intend on seeing her ever again. She was already packing her shit to go...somewhere. She'd figure that out tomorrow.

"I—Okay. Okay, but... Shit. My job is on the line here. Surely there's something we can do."

Do? What the hell were they supposed to do?

"Well you can't make her not have cheated on me, right? I'm sorry, but I'm not coming."

"I...wait. I know. I've got it." Bryan paused, and she was about to say no again when he started taking a hundred miles an hour. "Yes. Come anyway. Just you, okay? Come have a wonderful resort vacation on us like you planned. You can ski, you can relax in the hot tub, all your meals are paid for. Free wine. Spa treatments. All I ask is that you let me take a few pictures like we'd talked about when you won the trip. Some promotional photos, that kind of thing. That's all. You can do that, right? Just some PR?"

She wanted to say no, but he kind of had her at free wine. She needed to get out of New York, clear her head, figure out what her next move should be. Why not do it at a fucking spa resort and get pampered while she was at it? She could handle a few pictures. No problem.

She took a deep breath. "This will keep you from losing your job?" It made no sense, but whatever.

"Yes. Yes, please say yes." He couldn't fake that sort of desperation.

"Okay. Yes. I'll come."

"Next weekend, as planned?"

"Next weekend. Friday. Like the paperwork says."

"Perfect. You rock. I'll have a car pick you up at the airport. You've saved me. Thank you."

And then there was a click.

She stared at her phone where it sat on her desk, completely baffled by that entire conversation. She didn't understand. But then, she didn't understand a lot of things. Like how you sleep with someone for three years while you're in love with someone else.

Well, fuck Josie. She was going to soak in a hot tub, drink free wine, get a facial and take some hot woman back to her hotel room. A different one every night. That would show that cheating bitch.

Sure, she should have maybe planned things a little better. Like, maybe proposed earlier. But she'd assumed... well she'd assumed wrong. But she hadn't expected to win the damn "Honeymoon in Heaven" contest anyway.

Lesson learned. No more honeymoons.

She'd take a few days in heaven though. She could use them. She pulled out her phone to let her bestie know with a text.

> I called and talked to the Summit Springs people and decided to go alone. Don't make it weird. I need some time by myself.

Ginny answered back in less than a second.

GINNY

WHAT OMG IM CALLING!

Then the Macarena started playing.

"Hey, Macarena!" She smiled at the FaceTime call. "I said don't make it weird."

"I'm not. Are you okay? Are you going to do something stupid? Can I come?"

"I'm mad and heartbroken and completely fine. What are you wearing? Are you going out? Do you have a date?" She wasn't fine, but she wasn't in the mood to deal either.

"I am. She's a stud—a chef. I'm wearing something warm but cute. Low cut, but with a scarf."

Ginny was hot and only kind of knew it. What she thought was cute, most people would drool over. "You look amazing. I love your hair. Go make yourself her favorite dish."

"I intend to. I need that Christmas Eve girlfriend, girlfriend." She gasped. "Oh, god. That was tacky."

"So tacky." But she giggled her head off. She missed Ginny. They hadn't lived in the same place at the same time since college, but they'd always kept in touch. "Girlfriend."

"I love you, honey. Call any time except for after nine tonight. I hope to be busy."

"Nighty, you. Who needs sleep? Love you." She gave Ginny a wave and they both hung up.

Seriously, who needed sleep? She hadn't slept well in a week. A nice soak in a hot tub should help, right? She went to pour herself a glass of wine and think about what to pack.

2

"No, Idina. The death card simply means change. Please don't stress it. You've been looking for a new career. This is a great sign." Bekka shook her head and smiled, even though her client couldn't see her over the phone. "Please breathe."

I love my clients. They pay my rent. They keep me in clothes and Swiss cake rolls. It was a mantra Bekka used...pretty much daily.

"But Bekka, honey. What if I have cancer? What if I die? What then?"

The temptation to point out that she was a tarot reader, not a minister, was huge, but it didn't help. "Breathing, remember? In and out."

Her personal cell vibrated in her pocket, and she glanced at the time.

Dammit. She had gone over. Again.

"I have to run, Idina. You have a blessed day, and I'll talk to you in two weeks. I can't wait to hear about your new job! Bye!" She hung up before Idina could distract her.

She sighed and leaned back into her overstuffed couch-bed-office situation. Life was expensive, but she was free and happy,

Not in love, but that was okay.

It wasn't in the cards.

Her phone buzzed again, so she grabbed it. Everyone knew she was working, so it must be serious.

She flipped a card. Huh. Page of Cups. Must be—

"Bry! How's the ski mountain business treating you?"

"Great! I'm about to give you a two-week all-expenses-paid vacation to Pines Peak, and you're going to say yes to everything I ask you because you're my sister, and you love me." Bryan took a breath. "Please."

"What? Why? What happened? Are you okay?"

"You know that big honeymoon package contest I ran to try to impress the higher-ups?"

"Yes." Bry had been talking about it for weeks. She knew every detail. She'd seen every social media post and heard every satellite radio spot. She knew every single activity, perk and amenity that came along with the package, right down to the champagne-filled honeymoon suite featuring a luxury King bed and the hot tub on a private balcony with a view of the snow-capped mountains. "I remember."

"The one that ran for weeks and weeks, and we got thousands of entries?"

Really? "Mhm."

"The one that I was hoping would get me a promotion? That one?"

"I know, Bry. I know. Big, big deal." She smiled, hoping that he would be able to hear it in her voice.

"Are you ready for this? They're not getting married. The winners. They didn't get married."

"Oh, god...what happened? When did you find out?

That's awful!" A little bit funny, maybe, but she'd never let that out. She wasn't the marrying kind.

There was a short pause, and Bryan's voice was calmer when he answered. "I don't know. Shit. That has to suck, right? I was kind of pushy with her on the phone, I hope I didn't...wow."

"You didn't...pushy? I—What?" How could he have been pushy with a deserted bride? Or groom? No, he said she, that was bridey.

"I... I talked her into coming alone."

Okay, her brother had done some dumb shit before, but this was special. "That...how's that supposed to make things better? Reminding her that she got broken up with."

"Look. You can scold me later, okay? I need a favor."

"Okay. Sure. What? Do I still get a vacation?" She had her priorities, after all.

"Yes, early! Can you come Friday? I need you to...uh." Bryan sighed in that way he did when he knew he was in trouble. "I need you to pretend to be her wife."

"Pretend to...what? Bry. Bry, that's skeezy." And she wasn't skeezy, dammit.

"Oh my god. Bekka. No. Not for real. Just for pictures. Promo stuff. Smile and look happy. You know?" Bryan cleared his throat. "Save my job?"

Oh, that wasn't fair. At all. She pursed her lips and stared out of her studio apartment window, hands shuffling her deck idly. The six of pentacles landed on the table.

Huh.

Giving and receiving. Okay, that was a positive sign. "Do I get my own room?"

"Of course. I promised her some time to herself, you know?" Bryan answered her quickly. She hated that. That was the voice that got her grounded for stealing the cookies off the counter and eating them under the bed with him. That insisted that Mom and Dad wouldn't care if he snuck out and she covered for him.

"Bry—"

"Beks. Beks! It'll be fun. You get all these free activities and food and spa treatments and all you need to do is get your picture taken with this woman a few times. It'll be hilarious. It'll make a great story. I need my job, Bekka. Please?"

"I swear, Bry, if I end up getting in trouble or crying or... anything, I'm going to beat you." But she wasn't going to say no.

"You're going to have the red carpet rolled out for you and have some goofy fun. I swear. Thank you so much."

"You totally owe me, but send me the deets."

"I do. I owe you. I'll come be your plus one for the next straight wedding you're invited to. Deal?" Her phone chimed with an incoming email that Bryan must have typed up before they even got on the phone.

"Uh-huh. And you have to tell Mom I'm wildly successful too."

"Wildly. There's a herd of people with lots of money needing your insight and lining up at your door every day." Bryan managed to sound sincere and not sarcastic.

"Thank you. I'll pack warm clothes."

"Some nice things too, huh?"

"Okay..." Define *nice*.

"Okay. Okay good. Friday then. Send me your flight info, and I'll send a car to the airport. It'll be good to see you." Bryan was sweet that way, and she believed him. Even if the circumstances were suspicious.

"Sure. Sure. I mean, who wants to be here during the holidays?"

"Exactly! You're the best. You really are. I love you."

"I love you, even though you're a dork." Oh, who was she kidding? Bekka loved to go and do and see. There was a reason her life was footloose and fancy-free.

She couldn't wait to get away.

3

Marissa peered out the window of the limo as they left the airport behind. As vacations went, this one was starting out well. A little lonely maybe, but well. She'd had a first-class seat on her flight, which took off on time and landed early, and the limo driver had been waiting for her with one of those boards with her name on it.

Fancy schmancy.

And now she was being treated to an amazing view of the mountains from the highway.

"You'll find drinks in the cooler on your right and the controls for the satellite radio are on your left."

She glanced over at the driver who tipped his hat in the rearview and took his suggestion.

Half an hour and two mini bottles of chilled wine later, they were pulling into the resort as she sang along with the radio.

A weirdly familiar man came up to the limo, sharp features and copper penny hair making him seem like the world's biggest leprechaun.

"Mrs. Martin. Welcome. Your wife has checked in

already in the honeymoon suite, and you two have a champagne repast to hold you until your supper reservations."

Repast? People said things like *repast* out loud? Champagne sounded good though. "Honeymoon suite." She grinned at him. "I don't have a wife, but I'll take the champagne."

Wait. Did he say someone had checked in?

Josie?

Oh, she was going to hurt someone if they let that bitch into her suite. This was not a honeymoon, and Josie didn't get to be cute.

A key card was pressed into her hand. "I'm Bryan, head of marketing. Please, let me show you to your rooms. I'll get your luggage."

"Oh you're Bryan? Thank you." She let him get her things, but she was steeling herself for a fight. A slightly tipsy fight.

"I am. Let me get the elevator." He held the door open for her, then shut the door behind them quickly. "Thank you so, so much for playing along. I appreciate it."

"Playing along...yes." Oh, thank goodness. "Wait. So no one has checked into my room?"

"It's a suite, and my sister is going to be playing your wife for the week. She's harmless, pretty enough to look good in pictures, and willing to help."

"I'm sorry, I thought you just said your sister was playing my wife...?" What in the hell had she gotten herself into?

"Yes... For the promotions?" He was looking at her like she was crazy.

"I said we could take pictures. I don't remember saying I was going to pretend to be married..." Had she? She shouldn't have had that wine in the limo. She wasn't thinking clearly.

"She's just here for the pictures and the sponsors, you know? Just to make it look real."

"Sponsors. Right. As long as she's not in my hot tub it's all good." She'd make it work. She could smile and fake anything.

Though maybe not as well as Josie had.

She shook her head and followed Bryan. Forget that. She was going to be in a good mood. There was no way she was going to let Josie interfere with her relaxing week off.

"I'll make sure to tell her to stay out. She's just here as a favor to me."

"Uh-huh. Did you tell her she was saving your job too?"

"I did. She's good to me. She's got a job with a flexible schedule, so it makes it easy."

"Me too. It is handy, for sure." They went down a hall, up an elevator and down another hall.

"This is it." Bryan opened a set of double doors into a large open living area that was rustic chic—lots of stone and wood, but without that heavy log cabin feel.

"Oh wow. Nice." She wandered in, looking around.

"Here's the bedroom." He threw open a set of doors, showing off a huge bed, covered with white rose petals, a bottle of champagne and a tray of goodies waiting.

She laughed loudly at the idea of a rose petal-covered bed for one. "Very nice. Is this my *repast*?" She rolled the r, just to be silly.

"It is. Do you mind if I snap a photo of you and Bekka having a toast?"

"I guess not. Can I have a second to freshen up first? I must look like death after that plane ride." A couple of pictures and then she could have the night to herself.

"Of course. Please, take your time. I'll go sit and talk to Bekka. She's in the other room."

She took her suitcase and rolled it into the bedroom. "What's her room number? I'll come by when I'm ready."

"She's through the connecting door. Just knock."

There had better be a lock on that door.

"Fine. Will do. Give me a few minutes." She closed the bedroom door leaving Bryan on the other side.

Ginny was going to laugh her ass off and then remind Marissa that she been warned. So, maybe Ginny wasn't going to find out about this part.

Who was she kidding? She told Ginny everything. And this was their thing—she did something stupid, and Ginny said "I told you not to do that stupid thing" and then they laughed for an hour on Zoom while drinking wine.

She washed her hands, touched up her makeup, and shook out her hair, then put on more deodorant. She changed into a cute but comfortable dress and pulled on a chunky cardigan over it. When she felt good enough for a camera, she found the adjoining door, and discovered that it did have a lock on it, but it still felt too close for comfort. She opened her side and knocked.

"Coming!" The door swung open, and Marissa knew instantly that the world hated her.

Standing there was the gamine, wild woodland creature of a minx that she'd dated in college.

Rebekka Harker.

Fuck me.

Though it did appear that Beks had combed her hair today.

She ignored the instant tingle of attraction as the little hairs stood up on her arms. She had a type and, as appearances went, Beks was pretty much the sweet spot.

Damn it.

She rolled her eyes and snorted a laugh. "Really? You're the sister?"

Bekka's eyes went wide, and those pretty lips popped open. "Well, motherfucker."

Yep. Same filthy mouth too. This was beyond ridiculous. "You agreed to take fake honeymoon photos? *You?*"

"I did. My brother needed a favor. He didn't tell me the most—the most challenging human on earth was going to be here."

Challenging? Rebekka was essentially feral. "Well, he didn't tell me I was going to be posing with a Neanderthal."

Bryan stared at both of them like they were playing tennis. "Bekka, just shut up, take a picture holding the fucking champagne, and help me. It's not my fault the wedding didn't happen, but it is my job!"

Marissa glared at Bryan. "It's not *my* fault the wedding didn't happen either, just so you know. Let's get this damn picture over with. My champagne and hot tub are calling me." She turned around and moved back into the room.

"I didn't know you knew her?" Bryan whispered, and Beks hissed back.

"I don't know every lesbian in the country!"

Marissa snorted. "Your sister is an introvert. She doesn't know anybody."

"My sister runs a successful business. She's got tons of clients. Are you sure you've met?"

"Oh, I'm sure. She has a little moon-shaped birthmark on her ass." She picked up the champagne. "And she bites."

"Oh, my god!"

"Yep." Beks unbelted a huge, Bohemian tunic, letting it float around her. "Let's do this. Keep my face out of the pictures."

"I can say that? No face? I don't want my face either." She wasn't entirely sure she could muster up a genuine-looking smile right now anyway. She stood near the end of the bed, champagne in hand, and looked out at the view, which was spectacular. Mountains, snow, blue sky... "That's pretty."

"Bekka, hold the glass close. It looks romantic enough for Instagram."

Beks lifted the champagne flute, tilting it toward hers. "Like this?"

"Step a little closer together?"

She took a step closer and absolutely did not fondly remember how Beks smelled like incense and essential oils.

Not.

Damn it.

"Good. Good. That's perfect. Let me get a couple."

Beks was still, but not stiff, and her long, dark hair brushed Marissa's fingers.

She kept still because she was told to and focused on the hot tub sitting right outside a set of double doors that led to a small, private deck. She was going to sip champagne, rekindle the buzz she'd had when she got out of the limo, and search her phone for the best bars and hang-out spots at the resort.

There had to be somewhere for apres-ski yumminess. Everything she'd read about this town said it was lesbian friendly, with a number of welcoming businesses.

"That's really good, you guys. All done here."

"Great." She relaxed and set the champagne down in the ice bucket.

"So, tomorrow you'll get your lift tickets and rentals for the week, and then you have a complimentary couples ski lesson. I'll come to that to get some more pictures."

"Couples..." She sighed. She could probably use the

lesson; it had been a while since she was on skis. But did she want to make a fool of herself with Beks?

"I'll do my best to break something before the lesson, just to make it easier on you."

"Fantastic. If you don't make it downstairs for our romantic dinner for two that would suit me just fine as well." She didn't even know if there was such a thing, but she liked the snarky retort anyway.

"Actually, the romantic dinner is in the suite, just let me know when you want it scheduled. It's catered. And thanks for reminding me, I'll need pictures then too." Bryan was starting to get on her nerves. Or maybe it wasn't really Bryan, it was just this whole…debacle.

She should have said no to all of this.

"Jesus. Really? Well, if you don't need a picture of me taking off my dress to go sit in the hot tub then you can be going now," Marissa said.

"I need to rent a car, man. I'll go down the hill into town, and let the diva have her space."

"I'll give you my keys, Bekka. No worries."

There had been a time when being called a diva hurt her feelings. These days, Marissa owned it, even though anyone that really knew her only used it to be funny. "Yes, leave the diva to her spacious solo vacation suite so she can pretend like she wasn't walked out on. Thank you!" She herded them both toward the adjoining doors. "Goodbye. Again."

Bryan took Bekka's arm, voice low. "Jesus. What is the tea between you two?"

"She's stuffy. I'm me. I'm going to go down to the town and get a room. She's got shitty energy. Obviously she's in a terrible place."

"I heard that. And I'm allowed to be in a terrible place. And you're the last person I expected to run into here. Or ever." Maybe she just needed to relax and get over herself. She'd left New York at some ungodly hour, and it had been a long day.

"No one planned this, Marissa. No one. We're just trying to roll with the punches." When the fuck had Beks become reasonable?

"Okay. Well, forgive me if this particular punch—and I'm not talking about you—is more than I can really just roll with today. I'm tired. Maybe tomorrow. Have a good evening. Thanks. Goodnight." She closed her half of the adjoining door.

"Hot tub here I come."

4

"What the fuck were you thinking? You didn't tell her you were hooking her up with someone for the week?" And it had to be her "You're too much of a flake to commit to" ex-girlfriend Marissa Martin, didn't it?

Bekka couldn't believe her reading didn't come up with the three of swords, the tower, the fucking Queen of Swords in reverse. Anything.

Bryan shook his head, protesting. "I'm not hooking her up. This isn't a hookup. I told her I needed her to take some pictures. It's the same thing I told you. I just didn't know she...you'd...you know. With her. How was I supposed to know that?"

"Well, I had no fucking idea. And it was college. Sue me." Bekka had never intended to see Marissa again.

"Why are you yelling at me?" Bryan sighed. "I mean, okay. I brought you here because I really want this promotion, so I need to pull off this whole marketing campaign I dreamed up. I'm sorry."

"It's not your fault. I mean...whoa, right? When did you let her know she'd won?"

Bryan thought it. "This spring?"

"And she's...just telling you now that the wedding fell through?" Didn't weddings take, like, forever to plan?

Bryan's eyebrow shot up. "Yes...which is weird."

"Like stupid weird. I mean, when Barb did her wedding, she had to get a venue a year in advance, the church, the band, the dress." Goddess, the drama with the damn dress...

"So she accepted a honeymoon before she planned a wedding..." Bryan crossed his arms. "Why would you do that?"

"Maybe she did, and it was a left-at-the-altar thing." Her eyes went wide at the thought. "How awful would that be?"

"She did say it wasn't her fault. Damn. I guess I understand why she's so—" Bryan waved his hand at the closed and locked adjoining door. "Like that."

"She's very high-strung and stiff. She was even in college." Bekka had been wildly in love, or at least she'd thought so. She just hadn't been able to give Marissa the whole 'solid, stable' thing.

"If this is too much, I get it. You could not do this. I'll figure something else out. Keep your vacation though."

"No. No, I mean...obviously someone was evil to her. I'm not. Evil. Mostly." Maybe she could even make it better. At the very least, she could have a little fun here.

"Mostly." Bryan laughed. "Okay, I have to run. Hit me up if you want to have dinner; I don't have any plans."

"I will. Love you."

"I love you. I'm glad you're here. We get to have Christmas together. There's a festival at the farm in town that you'd love."

"Sounds perfect." She was a sucker for goofy Christmas celebrations.

Bryan gave her a wave and left her alone in her room. It

had a great view; she could see the mountain and the snow, the blue sky and trees. It was so wintery and picturesque.

There was a balcony, and she stepped out onto it to see if she could see more of the mountain. She could so see why Bryan had moved out here. It was amazing.

Marissa was out on the balcony in a heavy robe and cozy slippers, dark hair up in a messy bun. She'd started up the hot tub and was looking up at the sky, arms crossed tightly across her chest as if she were chilly.

Bekka didn't know what to say, but whatever happened, she wasn't at fault. "It's pretty out here, isn't it?"

Marissa glanced over sharply, squinting at her for a second, then looked away. "Gorgeous. And cold."

"Yeah, but that's how Christmas is supposed to be. Not hot. Unless you're Brazilian or Australian or something." They were used to it, she guessed. Did Aussie Santa ride a kangaroo?

"Yeah, I'm not feeling Christmas this year, cold or otherwise." Marissa stuck her hand in the tub testing the water. "Just getting it over with."

"I'm sorry, honey. I mean, about whatever happened, that sucks." That was clear, right?

Marissa snorted. "Well, she isn't the first woman I've been with who wouldn't commit to me."

For a second Bekka thought Marissa had said committed, and she'd almost—almost, thank the universe at large—made a terrible comment.

Then she thought about getting bitchy, but there was no way at all Marissa was talking about her.

"There's champagne." Marissa pointed to the bottle on the edge of the hot tub. "I might have swigged it. Sorry."

"I've had a swig after you before. I won't stress it." She took a deep drink, straight from the bottle.

"Good to see we're just as classy as we ever were." Marissa kicked off her slippers, hung her robe on a hook by the tub and got in. She was wearing a white bikini that covered almost nothing but was just enough to count. Sort of. Bekka watched Marissa's long legs disappear under the bubbling water. "Oh. Okay. This was worth the price of admission," Marissa said.

"Well, there you go." Bekka was less of the OMG sexy body type and more of the curvy girl end, but that wasn't new.

Marissa still did it for her.

Marissa relaxed back, water up to her shoulders. "So the marketing guy is your brother? He's nice. A little needy, but nice."

"He is. He's a sweetheart. This job is important to him. He's trying so hard." And she had a soft spot for the little asshole.

"I won't let him lose his job. It's not his fault I'm not having a real honeymoon." Marissa closed her eyes. "It's really mine for being stupid and idealistic and entering the contest in the first place."

"Were..." She tried to keep on, but her teeth were chattering violently. "Let me grab my jacket?"

This whole jeans and sweater thing wasn't helping.

"Hey!" Marissa called after her. "If you want to come in I won't stop you. I'm sure you have the same amazing robe in your room."

"Yeah? Give me a few." She had a one piece in her suitcase, and she managed to get it on and her hair put up before she let herself start to panic.

This was just her being nice to an ex who was in a shitty spot. That was it. Just good karma. She started to reach for her travel tarot deck in her suitcase but stopped herself. Did she really want to know?

No. If it was a bad call she was going to do it anyway, so what was the point?

Marissa was relaxing with her eyes closed when Bekka stepped out in her identical thick robe and fuzzy slippers. The steam promised warm water and the view from next to the tub was even better.

She slipped out of the robe and into the water. The heat was so sudden and shocking her nipples went hard, and she gasped with the contrast as she forced herself down to her neck. "F-fuck."

Marissa chuckled. "Good, right? I may never get out, because that might be torture. There are some towels in the warmer, but I'm skeptical."

"This place is amazing." She had no doubts. Of course, she lived in Dallas in an apartment. All Texans dreamed of coming to Colorado. The old joke about Colorado gaining a thousand feet of elevation if the Texans all left was true.

"It's a lot prettier than New York, that's for sure. And I don't have a hot tub in New York either." Marissa's foot slid against her leg and pulled away quickly. "Oh. Sorry."

"No worries." She didn't jerk her leg up. She wasn't taking more than her space, dammit. "Do you like it there?"

"I did, yeah. Now it's... I don't know what it is now. It's *her* space. It doesn't feel like mine anymore." Marissa looked past her toward the mountains. "I'll get over it, I'm sure."

"I'm sorry. That sucks." New York seemed like a great big place for one ex to take over.

"Mhm." Marissa went quiet after that, and they bubbled for a while.

Bekka listened to the water, distant voices, and the occasional plane or bird or gust of wind. When the gust turned into a steady blow and the sky started getting darker,

Marissa reached for the towels in the warming chest next to the tub. "Jesus, it's freezing. What happened to my blue sky? Catch." A towel came toward her high enough not to land in the water. "Time to go in."

The urge to snap was huge, but Marissa was right. It was time. Bekka stood up, and the cold was so big she just sank right back down. "Wh-wh-whoa."

When she blinked her vision clear, Marissa was already wrapped in her robe, feet in her slippers and the towel wrapped around her head. "You okay? Hang on, I'll get your robe. If I think it's cold, it's got to be hell for Texans."

"It's cold." There was no thinking about it. None. Zero.

"I know. You need to get out." Marissa took her towel and held up her robe. "Your slippers are right there. On three?"

"On three." She met Marissa's eyes, held them. "Don't let me fall?"

Marissa's stared into her eyes for a second, then swallowed and shook her head no.

Thank goodness her nipples had a reason to get hard, right? She reached up and counted. "One. Two."

Neither of them said three, but Marissa helped her out of the tub, into her slippers and wrapped her in her robe so quickly it felt like magic. Marissa pulled the hood up over her head and looked at her again. "Good? Breathing? Not frozen?"

"Uh-huh. I mean, uh-uh." She shivered, gulping in air as they hurried inside. "Man, tell me there's cocoa or whiskey or coffee or something!"

"There's gotta be." Marissa closed the door behind them and sat her on a fancy chaise at the foot of a giant four-poster bed. "There's a bar...ah. Whiskey, coffee, and cocoa. I'll make us something."

"Oh, wow. All the options." She curled up in her robe. "You think my brother would notice if I stole this robe?"

"I don't know, but mine will be going in my suitcase. They're amazing, right?" Marissa turned the heat up and started making coffee.

"Wonderful. I could live in it, I swear." Goddess, Marissa was still so pretty...

Marissa added a little of the instant cocoa to each coffee and then poured in whiskey shots from the minibar. "This might be the most disgusting thing ever, or, I might have invented something awesome. Either way, it's whiskey." Marissa handed her a cup, then sat on the end of her bed, grinning. "You first."

"Oh, that's cheating." She went for it, though, and it burned happily all the way down. She imagined the second sip would be better.

Marissa's eyes were on her. "It didn't kill you, so..." She took a sip and hummed. "Oh, not bad. More chocolate next time I think."

"It's got a burn, doesn't it?" She licked her lips and took another sip. Yeah, the second sip was better.

"Might be the whiskey, might be the very mediocre coffee." It didn't seem to matter; they were both sipping it. "That warms you up though, right?" After another sip Marissa sighed and looked at her curiously. "So, your brother said you have a business now?"

"I do tarot readings for clients." And she wasn't ashamed of it, either. She helped folks a lot.

Marissa's head tilted. "And that pays the bills?"

"It does." And she had her Masters in Psychology, so she was qualified to be a counselor as well.

"It's great that you found a way to turn what you love into a business."

Okay, that was almost nice... "Thank you."

"Mhm." Marissa nodded and the room went awkwardly silent.

She stared into her cup, wishing she was like Sandra Bullock in *Practical Magic*, and could stir the concoction with her will alone. Wouldn't that just rock?

Marissa cleared her throat. "And you're...in Dallas now?"

"I am. Well, basically. Not the city limits. I have an apartment in Flower Mound. It has a balcony; there's a pool." It was comfortable and fine.

"Sounds nice." Marissa pulled the towel off her head and dark waves of hair fell around her shoulders. She stuck her hand in it and shook it out.

"What about you? What are you up to these days?" Bekka asked.

"I'm in marketing. I oversee an entirely remote art department. I'm in New York, and they're all over the place."

"That's cool. Do you like it?" It sounded like something Marissa would be into. Control. Being the boss. Being the head honcho.

"It's what I went to school for basically, so, yeah. It's good. Fun. Creative." Marissa stood up and dropped her empty cup in a garbage can. "That wasn't awful."

"No. Thanks." And that was her cue to stand up and go into her own space, she thought. "I appreciate you sharing your hot water."

"Sure. Glad I was there to fish you out." Marissa watched her, hands tucked into the deep pockets of their fabulous robes.

"Me too. I—" Bekka just didn't know what to say. *Do you want to play rummy?*

"Yeah, look. I'm sorry I was such an ass earlier. Whatever

happened with us was a long time ago. I'm really not that petty. I'm just not in the best headspace right now."

"No. No, I'm sorry your—person—was a jerk. That sucks." She didn't understand why someone would leave someone else at the altar.

"Yeah. Well." Marissa shrugged. "I uh…"

She waited for Marissa to continue for a second, and when she didn't, Bekka found a smile. "You want to play cards or something after I get out of my suit?"

Marissa smiled back warmly. "Thank you. I think I'm tired and still on East Coast time. Can I get a rain check?"

"Sure. I'm here until after Christmas. There's no reason to be in Dallas when I can be here." She wanted to give Marissa a hug, but she also knew better. "Sleep good!"

"Yeah, me too. I don't have any reason to be in New York…at all. You can kick my ass at rummy tomorrow night. It'll be just like our college days."

"Yeah." Well, college featured orgasms and a lot of Boones Farm, but that was just a detail.

"Great. Thanks." Marissa was moving them toward their adjoining doors with purpose. "Good night. I guess we're skiing tomorrow. See you then."

"Woosh, woosh." She was going to go downstairs and have supper. She needed more than a cup of spiked cocoa for her meal.

Maybe they'd go to the steakhouse; she hadn't eaten a meal with Bryan in eons.

5

Staying in that robe and ordering room service had been the best idea ever, but getting up early to go skiing was at best a five out of ten. It would probably get higher marks if she hadn't finished off that bottle of wine all on her own.

The hotel sent up a huge breakfast that was obviously meant for two to share, but she hadn't knocked on Bekka's door yet. She was going to be good and dressed before she made that mistake again.

She was proud of herself for sending Beks back to her room when she did. It wasn't easy after that whiskey went to her head, but the other things the whiskey was trying to convince her to do were so out of the question it was the only way.

One whiskey in a little hot cocoa, and she was thinking about everything from dropping her robe accidentally on purpose to pulling Beks into bed.

That was a hard no. Been there, barely survived that.

The sound of full-on diva belting came from the other room, Bekka giving her best Sara Bareilles. It wasn't bad, and there was nothing wrong with the pure joy in the song.

That was actually pretty cool. She didn't remember Beks singing before. She pulled on a fleece sweater, thermals and wool socks, and once she was dressed, she knocked on Bekka's door. "Want breakfast?"

"Come on in." She opened the door to Beks, who was wearing nothing but a sports bra and yoga pants, upside down and singing.

"Oh." *Jesus.* She let herself stare a second, because what fool wouldn't? "Bad time. Sorry. There's this big tray of food in the suite..."

"It's fine. I was just relaxing and preparing for the day." Beks moved, and all those lush curves made the most amazing shapes on the way down.

"Do you always relax upside down?" She didn't recall that from their college days. She remembered some hot acrobatics, but they weren't yoga.

"Only in the last few years. I have an aerial setup at home, which makes it easier."

That was a pretty picture, but she made herself ignore it. "Well, if you're hungry..."

"Sure." Beks rolled down and sat up. "Head rush!"

"O...kay." She left the door open and went back into the suite to see what they'd brought up. Beks didn't look like she was ready for skiing, but skiing didn't really seem like Bekka's thing anyway. It wasn't something you wanted to do upside down.

Beks wandered out, hair up in pigtails, wearing long johns that hugged every curve.

"Oh, look at you, all ready for winter." Marissa's fingers itched to touch that waffle-weave-covered ass, and she picked up the coffee pot to keep them busy. "Coffee?"

"Yes, please! I do love my morning caffeine."

Beks didn't sound like she needed caffeine one bit, but she poured it anyway and handed Beks a mug. "I think there are crepes."

"Ooh, fancy. Are they strawberry or Nutella?" Beks smiled at her, holding the mug and breathing deep.

"I don't know. Let's find out." She handed Beks a plate and uncovered the crepes. Her stomach was growling, so she was definitely ready. Along with the crepes there was sausage and bacon, yogurt and fruit, and some kind of egg bake that looked amazing.

"Dude. This does not suck." Beks snagged a piece of bacon and nibbled while Marissa filled her plate.

"Nope. Looks like Nutella, by the way." No bad there. She put a couple on her plate along with too much of everything else. She figured what the hell, she was only going to get a fake honeymoon once.

They had folded the delivery cart out into a little table, and Marissa put her plate down to pull up two chairs from around the room. "Do you ski?"

"Nope, but I'm totally willing to try. You?"

"Not in a long time and I wasn't very good at it, but I'm game."

"Well, we take some pictures for publicity, we take a free lesson, and everyone's happy. Boom." Beks got a crepe and another piece of bacon.

"Sounds good. Does the lodge have a fireplace? I want to sit by a big fireplace after and drink something hot." It just sounded good. Frozen pink cheeks thawing out by a fire while she sipped hot cocoa. She liked the picture.

"Bryan says it's less luxe than rustic comfort, but still four stars."

Whatever that meant.

"So...more lumberjack and less chalet?" She chuckled and sipped her coffee.

"Yeah. I mean, this is a lesbian wonderland, after all."

"Is it? I knew it was friendly, but a wonderland? I had no idea. That explains the photo shoots and the queer-themed honeymoon giveaway." Huh. Summit Springs *was* a lesbian wonderland. Who knew? She took a bite of her crepe and hummed. "Mmm. Oh. Crepes are good."

"Where did you see the contest? I assumed it was a queer-friendly space..."

"Online someplace. Probably Instagram. I just didn't think about it. I saw free honeymoon and entered." Like an idiot. Next time she'd wait until the woman said yes to ponder things like a honeymoon. "No one ever expects to actually win these things."

"Yeah. I get tons of requests from clients asking about the lottery. I'm not a fortune teller."

She laughed. "Is that what you tell them? Even if they pay you?"

Beks tilted her head. "Of course. It's the truth. They don't pay me to lie."

"Well, no." She wasn't going to pretend to understand what Beks did for a living. Maybe she was just too practical. She took another big bite of her crepe. "God, that's good."

"Yeah? I'm convinced." Beks took a huge bite of her own.

She watched Bekka's expression go all swoony and tried to ignore the almost orgasmic-sounding yummy noises.

Tried.

And failed.

Snow. Ice. Freezing cold. Skiing. Penguins.

That didn't work either.

"Gosh, I think I'm full." She picked her coffee back up and stood. "Are we late? We might be running late."

"Oh? Already? All right. Let me put my stuff on. I have ear muffs."

"I bet they're adorable on you." She went to get her coat wondering why the hell she'd let herself say that even if it was true. She grabbed her hat and gloves and stomped into some ridiculously chunky snow boots that she'd had for a thousand years.

She wasn't that desperate, was she? Did she need to be ogling an ex that really ought to stay that way?

Soon Beks came bebopping out in a rainbow snowsuit, beaver earmuffs, and a GoPro.

She really did look adorable.

Damn.

"You definitely look ready to go skiing in a lesbian wonderland." She pulled on her purple ski jacket, which was boring by comparison. She was glad she'd gone with a color instead of black.

"Aren't you cute? I love that color on you!" Beks started singing Christmas carols as she opened the door.

Beks was way more of a morning person than she was. Or maybe Beks was like that all day? She honestly couldn't remember. "I guess it's been my favorite forever." She checked to make sure she had her keycard, then followed Beks out. "Did your brother say where we're meeting him?"

"He said there will be transportation up to where the skiing happens."

"Fancy. I had champagne in my limo from the airport. We probably don't get that up to the mountain." She laughed. That would be all she needed. Her skiing was sketchy enough without alcohol.

"Nope, that's apres-ski, right? Hot toddies and mimosas and all?" Beks bounced, her pigtails bobbing.

"And a lumberjack-chic fireplace." She imagined pulling on one of those pigtails.

In bed.

Jesus Christ, Mari.

She told herself her nipples were hard because it was twenty degrees outside. "Does it ever get this chilly in Dallas?"

"Ha! It's eighty today. I checked. This is *way* more fun." Beks scooped up a handful of snow and tossed it in the air.

She managed to stay out of the shower of snow, but she couldn't help laughing. She wasn't a free spirit like Beks, but she had to admit she enjoyed watching.

"Can you imagine living here? I would be making snow angels every day!"

She snorted. "I'd be drinking Irish coffees." She didn't know if she could imagine living here or not. "Have you been into town? I feel like I should go check it out."

"I have! I went down with Bryan yesterday for steaks and a beer. It's charming as hell. Coffeeshop, bookstore—even a chainsaw artist." Beks nodded, so enthusiastic. "It's magical at night."

She was sold. Maybe she'd go down there later and look around. She'd never seen a chainsaw artist. "Sounds fun."

"Right? I peeked in the coffee shop. They have pastries!" Beks laughed as the snow began to fall again. "It's snowing! I want to go to a hot spring while it's snowing."

She just wanted to get these pictures over with and try not to die skiing.

A strange sort of alpine golf cart stopped in front of them. A woman in a green one-piece snowsuit with the resort logo on it smiled at them from the driver's seat. "Good morning, newlyweds! Ready for some fun?"

Beks wrapped one arm in hers. "We so are! The snow is utterly romantic."

Marissa was going to beat her.

"Utterly." She deadpanned, climbing into the back seat. She let Beks have the front since she was so...bubbly. Marissa felt like she was going to need more coffee to keep up.

"You're getting beautiful weather this week. Some snow, some sun, not too cold...are you here until Christmas? If you are, you should check out the tree in town and go to the bazaar."

"There's a bazaar? Oh my goddess! I totally love that idea. Tell me *everything*!" Beks grinned back at her. "I love the whole idea of Christmas parades and pageants and bazaars!"

She had to smile because the notion made Beks so happy, and honestly, Marissa was intrigued too. It did sound like a good time.

Their driver went on. "There are vendors and crafts, tons of food and music, dog sled rides and ice sculptures. It gets bigger every year. And it's all lit up at night, it's great."

"Ice sculptures? Oh, wow. I'm totally in. That's amazeballs."

Did Beks just say amazeballs?

The cart rolled to a stop right in front of Bryan.

"I've delivered your newlyweds, and they're adorable."

"Good morning, ladies." Bryan offered her a hand out of the cart, and she took it.

"Thank you. Good morning."

"Hola! How goes? This snow is wonderful, and I'm in love." Beks made everyone grin.

"See ya later, lovebirds!" The cart took off.

"Bekka, you are very...colorful." Bryan gave her an

affectionate smile. "The snow might complicate my photo shoot a bit, but let's get your gear, and we'll give it a shot."

"Woohoo! Snow bunnies ahoy!" Beks winked at her brother, then headed into the ski shop.

How had she gotten herself into this?

"Snow bunnies? Really? Just my luck to be pretend married to a morning person." She followed Bryan and Beks to the ski rental building where they were fitted for skis, poles, boots, helmets, and goggles. She didn't even want to know what all of this high-end gear would have cost if she'd had to pay for it so she didn't ask. The good news was that she remembered how it all worked and was able to step into her skis on her own once they got outside.

Score one for the city girl.

Beks was nowhere near as competent, and ended on her backside three times while she was trying to get her skis on.

You'd think Bryan would have stepped in to help, but no, he was too busy snapping pictures. She stepped back out of her skis and offered Beks a hand. "I got you. Line up your toe." She put the toe of her own boot up against the front of the binding to hold the ski in place and let Beks hold onto her shoulder for balance. "Good. Now drop your heel and put your weight on it." She waited while Beks snapped her heel into the binding. "Woo! You did it. Perfect. Other foot?"

She caught Bekka's eyes and froze.

"Please. Thanks. My butt's going to be black and blue soon..." God, she was pretty.

She'd kind of like to kiss that bruised ass and make it all better.

"Don't worry, I'm sure I'll have some spectacular wipe out and we'll be nursing our bruised asses together." She tore her eyes away because the image in her mind was way too X-rated for being this close, even if it was only twenty degrees out. She repeated the procedure with the other ski, and Beks was good to go.

"Okay. Okay. Okay, this is weird, but cool." Beks rolled her eyes but stayed upright.

"These pictures are great you guys." Bryan looked pleased. She didn't realize he'd been taking pictures of all of that. "I've got enough of this for now. Are you ready to meet your instructor?"

This was going to be interesting. She wasn't sure poor Beks was going to make it. She was ready for some fun though. "Sure."

"Kailyn? Your victims are here!"

This tall, red-headed goddess of a woman sauntered out with a blinding smile. "Bryan. Be kind!"

So every woman in Summit Springs was hot and extroverted? She made a mental note to visit again next winter.

"I'm Marissa. I've only done this a few times." She stuck out her ski mitten and bumped with Kailyn.

"So you're the newbie?" Kailyn smiled at Beks.

"Totally. I'm new to all things fun and snowy."

Kailyn checked all of Bekka's equipment, as if she hadn't done a perfectly good job of getting Beks squared away herself. "Okay..." Kailyn helped Beks plant her poles and winked at her. "Rebekka, right?"

Wait. That smile was flirty. That instructor was flirting with Beks. Beks was *her* pretend wife, dammit.

"I'm going just walk, and you're going to glide. Right pole, left foot. Ready? Glide."

6

S o, things to note.

One, skiing was harder than advertised.

Two, ski rescue people were incredibly hot.

Three, the urgent care in Summit Springs was super used to treating broken legs.

Like *whoa*.

Bekka sat at the bar at the lodge, looking at the bright blue cast on her leg, drinking a milkshake and watching the flames dance in the fireplace.

"Okay. Bryan is working on changing the hike tomorrow to a spa day or something later in the week." Marissa sat a bottle of Tylenol on the bar and sat next to her. "How did you end up here? You should move to the couch by the fireplace, so you can put your leg up."

"I was... I just sat. So, maybe I'm not a skier, huh?" She was an idiot, and now she had a medical bill to pay. *Yay*.

"Fortunately, that's not a requirement in your line of work." Marissa gave her a sideways grin.

"Nope. Now if I'd had broken a finger..." Or her psychic bone, then maybe.

"Come on. Let's move you and get you comfy. I want my spiked cocoa by the fire, and you need to put that leg up." Marissa grabbed her crutches and substituted her shoulder instead. "I've got you."

"This is so embarrassing. I mean, I made it down one hill..." And she'd hit a tree. Bang. Like full-force hit a tree.

"Well, if that damn tree hadn't jumped in your way you'd have been fine. Stupid tree." They hobbled over to some wide log-framed couches with big, thick cushions.

Marissa was careful with her, lowering her down nice and easy, and she didn't notice how good it felt, having that lean body touching her.

Nope.

No noticing.

"This is what trees are good for. Lumberjack-chic furniture. What was one doing on a ski slope anyway?" Marissa winked at her, lips pulled into a knowing grin as she set the crutches down alongside the couch. "I'm going to get a boozy cocoa, and something salty at the bar. I'll be right back."

Bekka had to wonder what salty goodness she would find. It was a fascinating thought.

Peanuts?

Popcorn?

Salted caramel something?

After a couple of minutes, big bowl of popcorn landed in her lap. "They took pity on you and gave me a whole bowl." Marissa shook the bottle of Tylenol at her. "Did you take some of these yet?"

"Not yet." She rolled her eyes, her cheeks on fire. "I'm like a bad cliche..."

"Nah. But this might make that morning yoga a

challenge." Marissa sat in a chair next to her. "Can you reach your milkshake?"

"Yeah, thank you. I feel like I'm in a bad Hallmark mystery." Really, it was more a rom-com, but she wasn't telling Marissa that. No way.

"I hope not because that would make me a suspect as the evil ex, and you know damn well it was a tree that was trying to kill you." Marissa chuckled and put her feet up on the coffee table, crossed at the ankles.

"You might have planted that tree there, but honestly you'd be the easy suspect." It would fuck with her vacation, but not in the good way.

"Yeah, maybe." Marissa sipped her drink. "Does it hurt?"

"It aches, but it's not as terrible as I'd expected." And the little cast was cute. Sorta. "You going to sign my cast?"

"Sure. I'll ask your brother for a Sharpie. That should give him a challenge." Marissa leaned forward and touched her arm. "Can I be honest? That crash was pretty scary. Are you sure you're okay?"

"Nope! But I will be." She would probably have a hard cry in a little bit.

"That's a very adult answer." Marissa leaned back in her chair and sipped her boozy cocoa, and they both went quiet, watching the flames in the fireplace. But after few minutes of that, Marissa set her cup down. "Do you want to get out of here?"

"Yeah. I guess so. I want to get comfy and be a schlub." It seemed fair. She had to be on crutches.

"Oh. I didn't mean... I was thinking maybe we could put your gimpy butt in a wheelchair and go into town."

"Do you want to? With me?" It was snowy out there, and she didn't feel particularly pretty or interesting.

Marissa looked around them. "There's no one else

sitting here, so I think I meant with you." She got a wink. "At the very least a slice of pizza and a beer would improve this shit day, don't you think?"

"Is there anything pizza and a beer won't fix?" Okay, that felt amazing, that Marissa asked, that she wanted to hang out.

"Then it's a deal. Let's head up and change and call your brother to send up a courtesy honeymoon wheelchair. I'm sure a place like this will have one; you can't be the first person to break something." Marissa took a big swig of her boozy cocoa and stood to relieve her of the bowl of popcorn.

"Thank you. I'm a little scared I'll crash down again." And embarrass herself by being...herself.

"After all that bendy flex stuff you were doing this morning, I'm not worried. But who wants to crutch all over town in the snow? Come on."

Marissa bent to help her up and she ended up staring into her ex's cleavage and inhaling a subtle perfume. Lavender maybe.

No licking. None. Because that would be inappropriate.

Fun, but inappropriate.

Marissa went to help her up and laughed. "Okay, you still have to help me, gimpy."

"What? Why? You're a stud..." She hauled herself up, though, letting Marissa steady her.

"I bet you say that to everyone who is taller than you." Marissa snorted. "Oh, wait. Everyone *is* taller than you."

"Don't make me head-butt you, Amazon-woman." It was a familiar tease, a weird and comfortable one.

Mari handed off her crutches and shook her head, smiling. "Some things never get old, huh?"

"Or they're good because they are old. Either way." She

loved the idea of jokes that were so well-worn you could put them on anytime and be warm.

Mari stayed right with her all the way to the suite. "You realize that all of your brother's promo shots are going to have to be from the knees up now."

"I know! Hell, he's going to have to photoshop out any bruises." Because she was going to be wearing a couple of those for sure.

Makeup would hide the ones on her face, though, so that should help.

Mari started giggling. "That's a honeymoon picture... fancy resort and one of the wives is covered in bruises. Maybe he could market that to the kinkier crowd."

Bekka blinked, then she cracked up, laughing so hard she almost fell over. She wasn't sure Marissa had ever said the word kinky before.

"Whoa." Marissa was still giggling but caught her and made sure she was okay before letting go. "No beer for you, you can't even stay on your feet when you're sober!"

"If you get me a wheelchair, I don't have to worry about it!" she shot back.

Marissa whirled on her and stared at her, then nodded. "This is an excellent point. Go change and, after I do, I'll get us a chair and a ride."

"Hey, thank you for...going with the flow." It was unexpected and appreciated.

"Your flow was always a challenge." She got a wink and smile, despite the sarcasm. "I like challenges."

If only Marissa had liked her. "That will serve you well in life, right?"

Marissa met her eyes. "Yes. I hope so."

"Me too." Marissa helped her into her room and helped

her find a decent shirt that went with her flowy skirt. So thoughtful.

"Let me find some jeans. I need out of these snow pants."

Mari hurried off and returned a couple of minutes later in jeans and a warm, fuzzy red sweater. She was talking on the phone. "Yes, thank you...perfect...bye." Mari hung up and smiled at her. "They're bringing up a chair and they have a shuttle to take us to town. How cool is that?"

"Perfect. You're beautiful." Mari had always shone in that color, and the way the knit hugged her body was delicious.

"I...oh. Thank you." Mari covered a fake cough, probably to hide her blush. It didn't work. "They said there's another shuttle from town up to the farm where the bazaar is if we want to go. It stops at the pizza place. I thought that was convenient."

"Yeah? You want to go tonight or is it a daytime-only thing? Do we know?" Bekka didn't care. She just wanted to hang out.

"They said it's both. I bet it's pretty at night, but we should probably bundle up. Let's see how much energy you have; it's not going anywhere. Or—it is, but not before Christmas." Mari chuckled.

She had to giggle, because that was so, so very Mari. "Bundling up. I can handle that. Should I wrap up my bare toes?"

Mari tilted her head and gave her a look. "Yes, Beks. Unless you want to freeze them off."

"Well? Any ideas? My socks won't fit over the cast, and neither will yours." Maybe Bryan had a...a...shit, she didn't even have an 'a'.

"Hm. Good point." Mari frowned for a moment, then grinned brightly and hurried back into her side of the suite.

She came back brandishing a fuzzy hat with a pompom on the top. "It's fleece-lined. It should work until we can get your something in town."

That was the most adorable thing she'd ever seen. She squealed and grabbed her phone, snapped a picture, and posted it to Insta. "Hashtag so perfect!"

Mari looked pleased with herself, and winked when someone knocked on the door. "Your chariot awaits."

"Woohoo! Honeymoon of joy." She grinned over and dared to pat Mari's butt.

SHE JUST TOUCHED MY ASS.

Marissa blinked but didn't let Beks see her face. She was going to ignore that, right?

Right.

Obviously.

It was her own fault, because she'd been flirting like an idiot even though she knew that it was a bad idea. She had no interest in rekindling anything with the Queen of Chaos.

None.

Well, mostly none.

Beks hadn't changed much. The broken leg was absolutely no surprise, for sure, that was classic Rebekka luck. But there was a maturity about her now that Marissa didn't remember from college, and she was more...friendly? Outgoing?

Confident. That was what it was. Beks was still wild, but she was way more confident, and confidence was sexy.

"Your chair is shiny and red. How festive." She got out of the way and let the resort medical staff get Beks settled in it.

"It's a chair of sparkly joy. Can I make my gorgeous Mari push me around?"

"I think that falls under the 'for better or worse' clause." The nurse grinned at Beks as she left. "You should be good."

She rolled her eyes. "Haha. I think you're enjoying this too much."

"What? I'm the limping wounded!" Beks was so pretty when she teased.

She tossed Beks a coat and fixed the hat over Bek's toes. "That needs duct tape."

"That'll leave a mark on my pretty cast."

Beks actually meant that, and it was adorable. "I don't have tape anyway, goof. Ribbon maybe. Something. We'll see what we find." She took the handles of the chair. "Are you ready?"

"I am! You make breaking my leg almost fun!" Nut. This woman was a—

"Oh, hey y'all!" A woman in jeans and pigtails ran up as soon as they came down the elevator. "I was so sorry to hear about your accident, and on your honeymoon, no less. I have vouchers for coffee and goodies at Caffeine Ivy's, the spa here, the bookstore, and the art co-op. Also, my wife and I want to offer you a winter sleigh ride. I'm Cheyenne, by the way."

"Marissa," She nodded a greeting. "And this is Rebekka. A sleigh ride sounds like so much fun, thank you." This whole honeymoon thing was going to be hilarious to tell people about one day.

"This place is magical, isn't it, Mari? Like seriously magical." Beks stared up at her, and the temptation to lean down and kiss her was huge.

Not wise, but huge.

"If you feel that way now, wait until you get in the sleigh.

And visit the bazaar. Town is beautiful all done up for the holidays."

"We were just headed there for some pizza." And beer. She really needed a beer.

"Have fun! Here are your vouchers. Everyone's excited to meet and spoil you." Cheyenne handed over a fancy envelope.

"Thank you. Sounds great." She took it and handed it to Beks to hold onto. "We'll call about the sleigh ride soon."

"It'll be uber-romantic. I promise."

Uber-romantic. *Whoa.*

Okay, so maybe they wouldn't call. This pretending to be married thing was getting a little intense.

"I've never taken a sleigh ride. Have you? I'll have to take a thousand pictures. This is amazing." Beks waved to Cheyenne. "Y'all rock!"

"Actually it does sound pretty cool. But I kind of feel bad that we're taking all this stuff for free, and we aren't really on a honeymoon." She pushed Bek's chair toward the shuttle they were taking into town, grinning. "Not bad enough not to get a free coffee though."

"We're here. We can pretend and make memories, right? Is that awful?"

It wasn't awful, it was just awkward. The lie she could handle because she had tried to cancel and was asked to come anyway. But spending all this time with Rebekka was...

Okay, so, not as bad as it would have sounded had she known Beks would be here. But way back when, she and Beks had burned bright in the bedroom and otherwise pissed each other off continually.

She was lazy, and Beks barely slept. She was practical,

and Beks read tarot. She was focused on a career, and Beks was always saying something would work out.

Never mind that they both got what they wanted, that was beside the point.

Unless it was the point...

"I'm up for making memories." She obviously had a lot with Beks already.

"Me too. They can replace the hurting ones. We'll have a new reading." Beks winked at her, staring at her upside down. "I pulled the Hanged Man this morning. Usually it tells me to shut up and listen. Maybe today it meant, watch out for that tree."

"Maybe it meant you can't see everything coming." She winked right back and rolled Bek's chair onto the shuttle's wheelchair lift.

"This is true, but I'm going to try!" Beks laughed, and Marissa had to smile.

It wasn't a long ride into town, but it was pretty. Snow and the trees and the blue sky opened up to a cute little town decorated with wreaths and garland, with shop windows full of fake snow and holiday cheer.

"Goddess, this is charming!" Beks stared out the window, lips in a bow. She narrated everything they passed, and it was, mostly, charming.

"Town Center," the driver said as he pulled over. "Do you need me to get you anywhere in particular?"

"No, we're going to wander. Thank you." They'd find their pizza along the way.

"Be careful. They've cleared the sidewalks, but there might be patches of ice."

"You're so sweet!" Beks blew the driver a kiss. "Anywhere we shouldn't miss?"

"Coffee shop. It has the best pastries."

It was cold. They were going to need a hot drink at some point. "Coffee is a must. Thank you!" Marissa gave a wave as the van doors closed, then looked around wondering which direction to go in. "Okay. We're here."

"We are. There's—everything. This is like Fredericksburg, a little. All the cutest little shops."

"Fredericksburg?" This trip to Colorado was pretty much farthest she'd ever been from New York since college. "Like, Denmark?"

"Lord and Lady, no. Texas! Down toward Austin, from me." Beks chuckled, the laughter setting her pigtails to bobbing. "I only live about six hours from there. My best friend and I go for the wine tastings."

"Oh!" She laughed. "Here I thought you'd become a world traveler." Best friend, hm? She didn't know why she was curious, but she was. "Best friend?"

"Yeah, her name is Angel. She's an ICU nurse. She's got three kiddos and another on the way." Beks grabbed her phone, showing a selfie of her and a surprisingly normal-looking woman in SpongeBob scrubs.

"She's pretty." What the hell? Why did she say that? And why was she feeling jealous of a woman she'd never met over a woman she wasn't involved with?

"She is! I met her in the hospital, and we hit it off. Her husband is super nice too. He's a software guy."

"Excellent." The pretty nurse wasn't queer. She pushed Bekka's chair along the sidewalk, and it seemed to roll pretty well over the little snowy patches. "Wait. Why were you in the hospital that time?"

"I donated my kidney to a fourteen-year-old girl, and I got an infection."

Whoa. That was...stunning. "Okay, that was about as far

from what I was expecting you to say as you could get. That's...amazing. The kidney, not the infection."

"I had it to spare, and she was dying. She's a swimmer, a cellist, she wants to go to Julliard. I had to do it."

"How did you meet her?" She rolled the chair up to a big glass window all decorated for the holidays with greenery and holly.

"I never have. I heard about her on the radio. I went in for a test to see that afternoon. It was fate."

Fate. That was so Rebekka. She wondered how well Bryan had taken the news, but then again, he was Bekka's brother. He couldn't have been as surprised as she was. "Beks, that's the most generous thing anyone I know has ever done. Honestly. That's amazing."

"Thanks. I haven't told anybody. You know. Angel knows."

"You didn't tell Bryan? Why are you telling me?"

"You asked." Beks blinked, and then her eyes went wide, her cheeks glowed bright red, then she turned to face forward, burying her face in the bright red scarf.

What was that about?

"So..." She changed the subject because she didn't know what else to do. "The windows are festive, huh?"

"They're gorgeous. The whole town is a gem." Beks glanced all around, a faint smile on her face.

"Are you cold? How's your foot? We should find you some socks." She rolled on by that window to the next one, trying to look like she hadn't noticed whatever made Beks blush.

And telling herself that charming blush hadn't made Beks that much more endearing.

"Do they even make huge socks?" Beks shook her head.

"Maybe here they would, since it's a skiing accident type of place."

"I don't know. Maybe we can just find some festive ribbon for your hat." She chuckled. "I'm glad we came out. It's chilly but it's such a nice day." The two them just sitting around the suite with time on their hands seemed...ill-advised.

Mostly.

Part of her insisted it would be more fun than she could possibly resist.

"It was a good idea. I was sitting there feeling so stupid."

She shook her head. "Nah. It's not like we were planning on doing a lot of skiing anyway. Now you have an excuse to sit by the fire, drink wine and eat for the rest of the week."

"And celebrate the solstice! I looked, and it's going to be a full moon. I bet it's beautiful on the snow."

"I'm always up for a party." That was such a lie. She was not a party person at all. She was the type who used work as an excuse for not being able to do things. But it seemed like something good to say. "Cherry's Pies. This has a good pizza look. Are you hungry yet?"

"Yeah. Yeah, and I could get in out of the cold too."

Oh, that leg had to be aching. Dammit.

"In we go." She stopped the chair by the door. "Hm."

A young woman came out as she was trying to figure out how to get Beks in and pointed down the side of the building with a smile. "Ramp."

"Ramp! Thank you."

"Man, it gives you an appreciation for disabled people, doesn't it? I mean, I feel like I should think about it more, but you get so busy, huh?"

"You used to tell me life throws things at you for a

reason." She rolled Beks around the corner and up the ramp where an automatic door opened for them.

"I still believe that with all my heart." Beks shook her head, snuggling into her scarf. "I don't believe in coincidence."

"No?" They got inside where it was warm, and the door closed behind them. "You think winning a honeymoon contest run by your brother, coming here single after my girlfriend left me, and running into you was all by design?" That was some bad design if that was true, she was mad now, but her heart had been broken.

"You don't have to look at it that way." Beks shook her head. "What if you won, and I'm here to make it easier? Give you something to do?"

Right, Beks was a glass half-full person.

Still, it was hard to argue with her logic without sounding like she was feeling sorry for herself. "Okay. Point taken. I think a cinnamon roll from the coffee shop would make it easier too, don't you?"

"Oh, I do love a treat. Did you want to order a whole pizza to share or a slice?"

"I could murder a couple of slices. Should we get one to share? I'm not a dainty flower when it comes to pizza." Even if it wasn't New York pizza.

"You guys need a seat?" The hostess smiled at them. "Just grab whatever seems comfortable. Maybe that one by the window? It might be an easier path."

She nodded. "Looks great. Thank you."

They got settled, and she looked at the menu. What the hell was a Colorado-style pizza?

"Does the menu say the pizza comes with hot honey?" Beks said. "That's new."

"Oh. No. *When in Rome*...does not apply in this case." She laughed. "I think I'm too New York for that one."

"Well, we're here. We have to try it. You want all the veggies and sausage? Ooh...they have one with meatballs!" Beks pointed at a pizza pan with a huge braided crust mounded with toppings. "Look at that!"

Okay, honey and meatballs sounded so wrong, but how could she say no to that face? "Go for it."

"Cool! I love new foods!" That hadn't changed. Beks had always been willing to dive into new things with utter enthusiasm.

She ordered beer to go with it so if the pizza didn't do it for her, she'd have that to keep her busy. The server took the order and brought them some garlic knots to start.

When the dust settled and the table went quiet between them, she leaned back and smiled at Beks. "You shouldn't be embarrassed you know, about the kidney. That was a really kind thing you did."

"I didn't tell you to brag. I just...you asked, so it was tell or lie."

"I didn't see it as a brag. You're right. I did ask. I'm glad you told me the truth."

"I'm not a liar. That's important to me." Beks reached out under the table and stroked her knee, just once.

Bekka's touch was hot, and Marissa froze, torn between pushing it away and taking it. "I never called you a liar."

"No, I know. That's not what I meant. I wasn't accusing you of anything." Beks removed her hand, and Marissa missed the touch. "Someone was awful to you, wasn't she?"

Sure, she'd been lied to, but she didn't mean to put that on Rebekka. "Sorry." She nodded and looked down at the table, gathering her thoughts and trying to hold back the anger. "She was cheating. And not one time, and it wasn't some terrible mistake she regretted. She'd been playing me for months. Maybe the whole time we were together. I don't even know."

"What a cunt."

The words shocked Marissa—both the speed of them and the tone. Beks was usually all positive, all the time.

So shocking, she had to laugh. "Agreed. A fucking cunt." And that was the first time she'd smiled about Josie in months.

"Well, we'll drink to you being free of that nonsense. Jesus, I can't imagine. Cheating on you?"

"I'm an idiot, obviously." Their drinks landed on the table and the server moved on without stopping.

"She's an idiot and a liar and a terrible bitch."

She raised her glass. "Here, here."

Beks clinked their mugs together. "May she have crotch rot, forever."

"When did you learn how to say the right thing at the right time?" Maybe Beks always had, maybe she hadn't been a very good listener.

"It's my gift, and I've trained for it a lot, believe it or not."

"I believe it." She didn't know how you trained for something like that, though. "It's pretty impressive."

"Thank you. Now, tell me about your job. Your space. Your world. It's more interesting than mine."

"Me? I just did exactly what I said I was going to do. I graduated, went to New York, and found my marketing job. I'm a creative director; I have artists and professionals working for me from all over the country. It's fun, and I love that people are from everywhere. I can work pretty much anywhere I want." She'd already started to wonder, even before this all happened to her, whether she wanted to stay in the city when she could live somewhere else and still make her salary.

"I think that's great. I can too—I mean, all my clients are online, and I can make my own schedule. It's so freeing."

It was hard to imagine that someone could honestly make a living reading tarot cards. It just felt so far outside reality. Marissa wouldn't have believed it was possible except that Beks had always insisted she would, and she had.

The pizza arrived with two little bowls of warm honey, and she shook her head. "I can't believe I'm going to do this."

"I promise it can't hurt." Beks grinned and grabbed a fork, digging right in. She took a big bite and hummed. "The sauce is sweetish."

Honey and pizza. Unsuspecting New Yorkers were having nightmares as she took a bite.

But it wasn't bad.

Sweet for sure, but it went with the sausage well. "Okay, I'm not hating it yet..."

"That's better than flat-out refusal. It's not everyday pizza. It's a calorie bomb wonder."

"Of that I have no doubt. Perfect *fuck that bitch anyway* food." She took another bite. The cheese and the crust were heavy, but she felt lighter anyway.

"Attagirl." The nod and the proud smile made Marissa straighten her spine.

"Try the honey with me, I'm not doing it alone." She chuckled and ripped off a piece of the thick crust.

It was a wheat crust, and the honey was echoed in the thick braid of bread. It wasn't exactly pizza, but it wasn't offensive. Just odd.

She chewed thoughtfully, watching Beks do the same. "I don't hate it, but I can't say I understand it either."

"No, but it's interesting and not gross..." Beks dipped again, catching a drop of honey on her tongue.

Oh, the things she could do with honey. And Rebekka.

Jesus.

That really should be her last sip of beer.

7

B eks couldn't remember ever having so much fun with Marissa, and they'd had some good times together.

They'd shopped and eaten, laughed and gone to the neatest little Christmas do with a band and craft booths and a huge tree.

It was sparkly and pretty and...magical. Snow was coming down slowly, the world was pure Christmas, and... well, the leg thing sucked a little, but that was life.

Something had changed. She remembered Marissa as a perfectionist, picky, more of a wine girl. But this Mari drank beer, and tried weird pizza, and didn't complain one single time about wheeling her around town or ruining her shoes in the snow.

This Mari let Bekka feed her bites of decadent fudge by hand and bought her a cashmere scarf that was so, so soft and the most luscious violet.

"The next shuttle isn't for a bit, are you okay waiting here? Are you cold?" Mari parked her wheelchair next to a bench under an awning where they were out of the snow and sat down. "It seems like it's actually warmed up a bit, doesn't it?"

"Yeah, this is amazing. It's like a little wonderland." Of course, she wasn't having to push Mari, so maybe...nah. It would still be cool.

"It's beautiful. Summit Springs is so cute and homey feeling, right? I loved the coffee shop with the fireplace...and that art gallery across the street. I bet it's neat to live here."

"I know! I see why Bryan moved up. I wonder how much a condo here is...it has to be better than Dallas." Less humid for sure, and friendly.

"He's nice. Your brother. A little misguided, but nice."

"He's a turd, but I suppose I'll keep him. He's really harmless. He just wants to be on the ski slopes, you know?"

"Well, he's in the right place." Mari looked at her with a curious expression. "This was really nice. Fun. I had a good time."

"I had a ball. Thank you so much. This has been an amazing turnaround of a day." She couldn't stop smiling, didn't even try.

The shuttle pulled up and let a few people off, then lowered the lift for her chair.

"That's our ride." Mari rolled her on and set the brakes. "See you inside."

"Okay."

"How you doin', honey?"

"I'm amazing." She was cold, her leg hurt, her butt hurt from the chair, her hair was wet from the snow—who knew snow was wet?—and she had to pee, but she'd never been happier.

Mari climbed into the shuttle and sat next to her, all smiles as they drove off toward the resort. "Warner in here, huh? My fingers are frozen. Feel." Mari took her hand and squeezed her fingers, then covered their clasped hands with her free one. "Oh. Yours are cold too!"

Bekka dared to tug up her sweater and press their hands on her belly. Her abs jumped and jerked, and her nipples went hard as diamonds.

"Beks..."

For half a second she thought she'd made a terrible mistake because Mari looked so shocked and confused. But that feeling of dread turned into something else entirely when Mari leaned over the arm of her wheelchair and kissed her. It was a confident kiss, the kind you got when someone knew what you wanted, not questioning at all.

She whimpered, opening right up to the flavors of peppermint and coffee and fudge and Mari.

Fuck, she remembered that flavor in the marrow of her bones.

Mari's fingers were warmer as they spread out across her belly.

"Aww. I remember being a newlywed. You two are so lucky."

Mari ended the kiss but held her gaze. "Very lucky. Glass half full, right?"

"Absolutely. Enough for a nice long drink, Mari." Bekka could sip from this particular glass for a while.

"You've warmed up." And so had Mari's fingers.

"You have that effect on me." In fact, Mari made her more than a little nuts, in the best possible way.

"Even after all this time?" Mari was still so close, leaning on the arm of her chair.

"You're still *you*, dork-woman. You still do."

"The same way you're still you, and also, different you. Or maybe I'm a different me." Mari shrugged and rolled her eyes. "If you know what I mean. You seem pretty warm now." Those fingers pressed against her skin like they were holding her in place.

"I do." Shit changed. Shit stayed the same. The changing of shit stayed the same. It was part of life. "Don't overthink it. We liked each other for reasons."

Marissa laughed at that and shook her head. "I overthink everything, Beks. That hasn't changed. I did kiss you first though, so I'm not completely hopeless."

"Not hopeless." In fact, Mari made her full of it, hope, that was. "It was a very respectable kiss."

"Well, we are in a van." Mari winked at her, fingers sliding over her middle.

"And your hands are warm now." She leaned into the touch with a hum.

"Mhm." Mari slid her hand away and sat back in her seat. "How does your foot feel? It must be cold too."

"My leg's a little achy, but the foot's okay. Chilly, but okay." She wasn't cold, deep inside.

"That festive ribbon we found to tie that hat on totally makes the look, you know." It was bright red with green Grinches all over it.

"I am super-duper classy, thank you." Bekka bowed in her chair.

"I love it. I really do." Marissa took her hand and just held it as they turned into the resort. "Your place or mine? Oh...it's the same place."

"It is! Look at that. We have a...a...a..." Goddess, what was the word. Not reason. Not excuse. She felt so silly, because she knew what she wanted to say, but she couldn't seem to get it out of her mouth.

"Yeah. We have that." Marissa kissed her again just as the van pulled to a stop.

Oh, they *so* had it.

And she wanted to have it again.

"OKAY, I'll be honest. Pushing this chair on the carpeting is a challenge." Marissa pulled Beks through the door into their suite and parked her. Thankfully, they'd stopped at the bathroom n the way into the hotel.

Beks blinked up at her, makeup all but gone, and smiled. "You're a stud."

She didn't know about that, but Beks had a way of making her feel confident. "This stud wants to kiss you again." She dumped her coat on the floor and braced herself on the arms of Bekka's chair.

"I am most certainly in, but first—" Beks locked the brakes. "No sending me flying and you hitting the ground."

"Where's your sense of adventure?" She leaned in, getting close enough to brush lips with Marissa. "Besides, how long do you think you're going to be in this chair?"

"Not long. I want to be in a bed with you, Mari. I want to play and see your lips part when you come."

Jesus, who was this Rebekka? She'd been untried, worried, and now she was a goddess.

She helped Beks get her coat and scarf off, then untied the ridiculously wonderful Grinch ribbon and tossed the hat into the pile of their winter clothing. "I've never fucked someone in a sexy blue cast before." She stuck out a hand to help Beks up. "Let's get you out of that chair."

"Thank you for today." Beks pushed up right into her arms, bringing their lips together.

Today isn't over yet. She lifted Beks out of her chair and set her down without breaking off their heated kiss and felt pretty smug. Maybe she was a little bit of a stud after all.

Beks hands slid around her waist, thumbs digging in over her waistband just enough to let her feel it.

She let Beks lean and held her up, coaxing her to open and let her taste. Beks was lush, meeting her passion head-on, and making Marissa feel like there was nowhere else she wanted to be.

She started yanking off layers—her sweater, then Rebekka's, her t-shirt, then Bekka's tank top, and finally got her fingers on the clasp of Bekka's bra...remembering well that next to Bekka's gorgeous ass, those luscious breasts were once her favorite thing ever.

"Mmm..." Beks had pushed her fingers underneath the band of her bra, fingers finding her nipples with unerring accuracy.

Still so damn impatient.

She unhooked the bra and then reached back to undo her own. She'd lost count of how many underwires Beks had snapped by not waiting just one...more...second.

Beks chuckled softly, like she knew just what Marissa was thinking. "I can't help it. You're irresistible."

"I'm not trying to change you." And she had a bigger budget for replacing bras these days. "Let's get you off your feet or...foot."

"Sounds good. It would kill the mood to land on it." Beks licked her lips. "I don't want to kill the mood."

Tipping over and landing on the floor would be totally normal for Beks and wouldn't kill the mood at all, but that didn't make it a good idea. She helped Beks over to the nearest bed, which happened to be the one she'd been sleeping in. "It's all part of the mood, pretty."

"Mmm..." Beks worked her jeans open, lips on her lower belly as she wiggled them off.

Warmth spread up her torso and electricity rippled deep

inside Marissa with those kisses. She took a shaky breath but it didn't stop her head from swimming. "Bekka."

"Uh-huh. You smell so good, Mari. I need you." Bekka's fingers slid into her panties, teasing and playing alongside her clit, but not giving her any direct pressure.

"Yeah." She pushed them down, kicked them away and leaned forward, forcing Beks to slide farther back on the bed using her good foot. Then she pushed Bekka's skirt up and tugged her panties down, working them carefully over the cast, stopping for just a second to tickle Bekka's toes before tossing those panties too. "You used to be so…" Shy wasn't the right word. Timid was wrong too.

"Innocent?" Beks teased. "Delicate? Untried?"

She grinned, hanging over Beks. "And now you're so… not. And I like it." She liked it a lot. She worked her fingers into the waistband of Bekka's skirt, but got distracted by those gorgeous breasts and her tongue darted out for a taste.

"Mmm…" Beks arched into her lips, the motion smooth and a pure plea. "Hot, Mari. Your mouth is what dreams are made of."

And Beks was addictive. The sudden memory made her ache. It was strange what bodies remembered that minds didn't. She sucked a nipple into her mouth and teased it.

Beks cried out, the sound soft as silk as it dragged along her back.

That was the end of her patience. She wanted to touch, to feel. Marissa slipped her hand between them as Beks had done earlier and found her ex-turned-new lover so ready for her. She dipped her fingers in gently, then circled that sweet little nub, knowing now, all of this coming back to her in a rush.

"Mari…" Beks bent one knee, spreading herself with an ease that spoke of knowing what she needed. "I need you."

She let the nipple pop from her lips and kissed her way over Bekka's tummy, teasing and nibbling along the way. She wasn't above a little happy humping when she was in a hurry, but they had all the time they wanted and nowhere else to be.

"No fair. I can't reach you too." Beks stroked her hair, fingers tangling and tugging, just the littlest bit.

She chuckled. Beks used to be perfectly happy to just receive. "Oh, well, don't let me be unfair." She reversed direction, nipping at the deep navel on her way to nuzzle between Bekka's breasts.

"Mmm..." Bekka wiggled down, bringing their lips together, fingers sliding in to tease her slit.

She moaned into the kiss and arched toward the touch, seeking more, wanting more than she'd expected. Beks was begging too, hips rolling toward her and she flattened her fingers, sliding them over Bekka's clit.

Bekka nodded, deepening their kiss, even as she set up a rhythm of gentle tapping and stroking, the action designed to make her dizzy. Between the hungry thrust of her tongue and the heady touches, Marissa was going to shake into pieces.

Her moan sounded needy even to her own ears as she hooked her heel around Bekka's thigh, body begging while her thoughts scattered.

Then Bekka slid two fingers inside of her, thumb pressing her clit and drawing lazy circles that threatened to steal her breath.

She did the same, though it was hard to focus on anything nuanced with Beks doing everything just right. It was sweet though, feeling Beks respond instantly. Her girl was wet and slick, no question how badly she needed.

"Want to come, then I'll make you do it again."

"We've got nothing but time, pretty." Her voice was wispy and she was so close. She rocked against Bekka's fingers and pushed hers deeper, palm pressing down to make sure Beks got what she needed. "God..."

"Right there. Right fucking there, Mari." Beks bit her earlobe, the little sting making her hiss.

She nodded because any second now... "Oh. Fuck." The dam broke, and she bucked into Bekka's hand, shuddering with her orgasm. Every touch after it set off a new wave, and Marissa moaned softly, heart pounding, trying to keep some of her focus on Beks and on giving her the climax she'd asked for.

Beks bucked and rolled, not passive at all, taking what she needed, demanding and hungry.

It was the fucking sexiest thing she'd ever seen.

"Come on, pretty. You're so close...almost there. Fuck, you're beautiful." The words flowed easily because they were all true.

"Mari!" Beks dragged her into another kiss, tongue fucking her lips as Beks shook and shuddered around her fingers.

Damn. She did a little battle with Bekka's tongue until she won, and Beks tremors slowed slightly. It was a hell of a kiss though, until she was forced to break it off so they could both catch their breath.

"I—Whoa." Beks panted for her, wiggling back and forth.

Marissa giggled softly and stretched out, offering Bekka a shoulder to lie on. "I needed that so fucking badly. Thank you."

"Me too. You feel perfect." Bekka cuddled right in, breath hot on her breast.

"You've changed. A lot." She didn't mean that in a mean

way, but she worried Beks might misunderstand. "I mean... You're so much sexier."

Beks nodded against her, cheek so soft. "I grew up. You were so much more mature than I was. I mean, I'm still not Sally Serious, but I know myself, know what I want."

That was clear. "You were such a nightmare." She laughed. "For me, anyway. I didn't know what to do with you."

"I just wanted you to like me. I didn't know that I had to like myself first."

She gave Beks a squeeze. She'd been popular, smart, pretty. People had liked her. That didn't mean she liked the person she saw in the mirror. Ironically, it had been Josie who finally taught her who she should love the most, long before they broke up.

"I like you, Beks. I like you a lot."

8

Bekka woke up, warm and naked and...her hair was caught under Mari's head.

Huh.

Also, vaguely ow.

And she needed to pee, and casts were heavy.

And Mari didn't seem to be going anywhere.

She traced one finger around Mari's nipple, watching it draw up, wrinkle as it tightened.

Mari licked her lips and hummed softly, eyes still closed. "Evil is as evil does."

"Mmhmm... I'm a very good girl." Totally good. Close to angelic, even.

Goddess, she was going to get zapped.

"Did you sleep?" Mari stretched and shifted, and suddenly her hair was free.

"Like a log. Are my crutches close, honey? I have to pee like a racehorse."

"Oh. Uh..." Mari sat up and looked around, then hopped out of bed and retrieved her crutches from her side of the suite. "Crutches." Mari seemed so comfortable being naked.

"Mmm...thank you." She stole a quick kiss, then limped and hobbled to the bathroom. She did her business and washed up a little before she crutched her way back.

Mari was giggling softly. "I don't know who decided that crutches were safer for you than being on skis."

"You just like watching my boobs as I jump along." She winked, cackling as she laughed.

"Oh, I'm not even going to pretend that I don't." Mari was all smiles and bedhead. "Is it morning? The middle of the night? I'm hungry, are you hungry?"

"I don't know, and I think so. Starving." Bekka's stomach was growling good and loud.

"Pancakes?" Mari picked up the hotel phone. "Sausage?"

"With lots of butter and maple syrup? Please?"

"Mhm. Hello, room service?" Mari ordered the pancakes, sausage, butter and extra syrup, a bowl of berries, coffee, juice and a bottle of champagne. "No, this isn't for breakfast later, this is for now. Mhm. Late dinner, early breakfast, call it what you like. Thank you so much."

That confirmed it must be the middle of the night.

"I think they think we're crazy." Mari grinned at her.

"We're on our honeymoon. We're allowed."

"Exactly so." Bekka got a playful kiss, and then Mari slipped out of bed and wandered toward the bathroom while finger combing her hair. "My turn, and then I guess we should at least find robes so we don't scandalize room service."

"Mmm... I can wrap up in a sheet like a toga, if you want." Bekka giggled, finding herself more than a little over the moon. She was naked. In bed. With Marissa.

This was a damn fantasy.

"Oh, like in the movies!" Mari called from the bathroom.

She heard a flush and water running for a while, and when Mari finally came out her hair was just about perfect. "Better. Took care of my pizza breath too."

She had wrapped herself up, and she imagined she either looked like Liz Taylor or a marshmallow.

"Mmmm-m. I have a Greek goddess...or maybe a sexy mermaid in my bed." Mari climbed back in, sitting close.

"Oh, mermaid. I like that. I like that thought a lot." She managed to keep the cast covered, so she didn't ruin the illusion.

Mari kissed her cheek. "What should we do today, pretty?"

"Mmm...can we make love again?" She'd suggest the hot tub, but hot tubbing in a garbage bag seemed a little tacky.

"Oh, that's already on the itinerary. Three or four times I think. But location is key. The shower's not a great idea, standing up seems like a mistake, the hot tub is totally out..."

"Yeah. I'm going to have to shower eventually." She cracked herself up. "Or I could just spread wide and dangle my leg out over the edge."

"Oh. Now, that's a picture. No bad there." Mari was giggling and smiling at her.

"You know it. I'd be presented to you on a bubbly hot tub platter." They both started laughing, and Bekka was in so much trouble.

"I'm not sure I'm that athletic. But I'd try. I would definitely try."

Her flush warmed her entire body, and she squeezed her thighs together at the look in Mari's eyes.

"My mermaid is blushing." Mari kissed her, sliding fingers into her hair.

Yours. Always, even if this is a fantasy.

She opened up, tongue sliding along Mari's.

She lost track of time as they made out and they were both startled by the knock on the door.

"Oh, shit. Room service." Mari jumped out of bed and tightened her robe. "You go back to looking perfectly disheveled."

"Right on." She tied her hair on top of her head, made sure the sheet covered her, but not too much.

Mari giggled all the way to the door and let room service in. The two servers were completely unfazed by their lack of dress and set their food up quickly.

One of them stopped on their way out the door and grinned at her. "Enjoy."

"I plan to." Mari chased her out and locked the door behind her.

She let the sheet fall a little farther, catching on her nipples, which were hard as nails. "Smells good."

"I am so hungry." Mari crossed her legs on the foot of the bed and started pouring coffee. "Still take it with cream?"

"You know it. I tried dieting. It didn't work for me." She winked over, licked her lips.

"Pfft. No. I wouldn't work for me either. You're perfect just as you are." Mari winked at her. "Well, maybe minus the cast."

"Yeah. Yeah, that wasn't my most graceful moment, huh?" But it had let her be closer to Mari, so she'd take it.

"I already told you, we're blaming the tree." Mari set her coffee where she could reach it, then dug right into breakfast.

"Totally. I tell you, it jumped out in front of me."

"That's the story, and we're sticking to it. Eat your pancakes. You need your strength." Mari winked at her. "Also, they're delicious."

"Everything with maple syrup is amazing." She dipped a bite in syrup and hummed over it, pondering how Mari would taste, with a light touch of maple.

Mari took another bite and watched her while she chewed. "I want to know...so much. What happened after college? Did you go home? How did you do this? Get your business going?"

Bekka licked her lips and grinned. "I went to grad school in Dallas, and when I was there I met a woman—don't all stories begin with, I met a woman?" She winked over, loving how Mari laughed at her. "She was a psychic, a tarot reader, a mystic, and she helped me learn about how we can communicate via alternative methods."

Mari rolled her eyes just like she always had. "The only alternate method of communication I need is the naked kind."

"That's totally fair, but that's not true for everyone, right? Some people need a way to talk out their issues. I provide that."

"I'm not saying they don't. But I'm not saying I get it either. Anyway, that's not my question. So you learned from a...guru?"

A guru. Oh, that was so Marissa—such a skeptic. "No. No, she's a professor. She was my thesis advisor, as a matter of fact."

"You were screwing your thesis advisor? Scandalous." Mari chuckled and picked up her coffee.

"What? No!" Her eyes went wide. She couldn't even imagine sleeping with Magda. "She's a grandmother of eighteen little ones. No, she was my advisor, my teacher, my friend."

"What? I'm sorry, you said you met a woman... I thought--" She could tell Mari was trying so hard not to laugh. "I mean. I assumed."

"She *is* a woman, but not a fuckbuddy, if you know what I mean..." She rolled her eyes at Mari. "I tended to find undergrads for those..."

"Ha! Taking advantage of the young and impressionable. I never would have guessed." Mari held out a bite of sausage. "Open."

She opened right up. She didn't take advantage. She just enjoyed the young and snuggling while she was recovering from Mari.

"Good, right?" Mari sipped her coffee again. "I'm not making fun of you, Beks, honestly. I'm really impressed, and I'm absolutely happy to admit I was wrong about you."

"You weren't that wrong. I was young and I needed to explore all my options. Now I know what I'm here for."

"I know what I'm here for too. I just don't know if I can do it where I was anymore."

"Do you not like it? I mean, New York?" She didn't have an opinion on it; she was more curious.

"I love New York. But New York is Josie now."

"Oh." Yes, that made sense. "I can see that. I'm so sorry. She sucks."

"Well, she's making someone happy I guess. I like to think I dodged a bullet. I can work anywhere. My whole team does."

"So, where would you go?" She thought she might see if she could find a little place here. Colorado was expensive, but worth it.

"I don't know." Mari shrugged. "I'm not there yet. I have no idea."

"That's fair. I can do a reading for you later, if you want." She found that it clarified a lot.

Mari snorted softly and shook her head, but then turned and looked at her suddenly. "You know what? Why not?"

"Cool." She fed Mari a bite of pancakes to muffle the urge to squeak.

"Mmm." Mari chewed and swallowed, then smiled at her. "What do you usually do for Christmas? Most of the time I'm working right through it. It's going to be nice to just relax."

"Sometimes I go on a cruise, sometimes I go to friends. This is a busy time for Bry, so it's neat to get to see him, take a break." She tended to be busy with some clients in crisis, but this year, so far, it had gone well.

"Does he have a family here? He seems pretty invested in the place."

"He's dating a little ski bunny who travels all over teaching skiing in the winter and doing rafting in the summer." He was happy seeing her a few times a month. They had an exciting relationship.

"Well good for him. Does he have a place here? Or an apartment at the resort or...?"

"He lives here in staff housing. It's a cute little apartment. Tiny, but free with his salary, so he's good." She got it.

"Can't argue with free." Mari flopped back on the bed with a groan. "Oh, that was so good. Yummy."

She reached out, parting the robe and stroking Mari's belly. Damn, that was the prettiest little stretch of skin.

Mari tangled their fingers. "Let's sleep in and bum around the room tomorrow. A day in. What do you think?"

"I think that sounds like heaven. I would love to spend

time with you." Bekka blushed dark, but it was the truth. Mari fascinated her.

"Rest your foot. Make Christmas plans." Mari kissed her fingers. "Screw around."

"I'm in, Mari." She winked up, circling the sweet dip of navel. "All in."

9

Marissa had spent most of the day enjoying Bekka and not caring what time it was, but they had dinner reservations in the swanky resort restaurant, and she'd sent Beks off to her side of the suite to get dressed half an hour ago.

She'd showered and done her hair, blown it out and left it down, but now she was thinking she should put a clip in it, like a half up-do. Something about the dry air here made it staticky.

Her wardrobe was on point though. The skirt was a little tight and her blouse was a little loose in all the right places, and she was wearing the one pair of heels she'd brought with her.

She knew that wasn't Bekka's style, and she didn't care. She liked how she looked, and she knew she'd love Bekka's look just as much. They were so different, but so...right anyway.

For now.

Maybe longer if...well. Maybe.

There was no telling with Beks, honestly. She could

change with the wind. It used to drive Marissa crazy, but it was part of Bekka's appeal now. The free spirit was... beautiful to her now in a way that it wasn't before.

She pulled up the front of her hair and pinned it back in a clip, smoothed her eyebrows and gave herself a wink.

Bek's was waiting for her in a lace peasant blouse and a long, multicolored broom skirt, her hair was braided into one long, thick hank with a band of flowers fastening it off.

She felt her smile turn fond, affectionate, and wondered why she'd never appreciated Beks this way before. "Hey, beautiful."

"Look at you!" Beks beamed at her. "You're stunning. How am I supposed to keep my hands off you?"

"Pfft. You're not!" She went right to Beks and kissed her. "You are a goddess."

"You know just what to say, don't you?" Beks reached up and drew her back down for another kiss.

She hadn't thought about how spot-on that was, but it was sincere and she made sure Beks knew it, leaning into the kiss, glad she hadn't bothered with lipstick.

Bekka's lips were soft, warm and open, and she smelled like sandalwood.

Marissa had spent all day with her hands all over this woman and she wanted more. But she was also looking forward to a night out, a little red-carpet treatment, and some dancing, so she let Beks go, took a step back, and offered her arm. "Are you ready for some fun?"

"I am!" Beks hauled herself up and grabbed her crutches. "Let's go paint the town."

She got the door and held it open until Beks got herself through it. "You're sure you don't prefer the chair?"

"I'm good. I'm feeling way less shaky. Seriously. Is the cast ugly?"

"What cast?" Marissa walked with her down the hall. "All I can see is how gorgeous you are."

"Perfect answer, perfect body." Beks laughed for her, moving with surprising grace down the hall.

Not perfect, but she was glad Beks thought so. "You're already getting better with those things. You have a little crutch-swagger going on."

"I've got good muscle memory, you know?" Beks shot her a wink.

She chuckled softly. "Must be all that yoga." Had to be something, Beks was limber as hell. She hit the elevator button. "The restaurant is the other direction from the lobby off the elevators, they said it was close."

"Cool. I met the chef. She's a hoot. A real toughie, but she had a warm smile. Deidre, her name was."

"You did?" The elevator doors closed behind them. "You're so good at that. Talking to anyone."

"That's the Texan in me. It's a habit of geography, right?" Beks chuckled—at herself, Marissa thought.

"New Yorkers talk. It's swearing mostly, and not meeting people's eyes on the sidewalk, but it works for us."

"I like the way you talk to me," Beks said, voice soft and gentle. "Quite a bit."

Mari smiled at her and then the grin turned wicked. "Even when I'm swearing?"

"Maybe especially when you're swearing..." Beks waggled her eyebrows, so evil.

"M-hm." Mari was laughing when the hostess came to seat them.

"We have a—"

"Oh, I know who you are. We've been waiting for you two." The hostess picked up two menus and led the way, slow enough that Beks could follow easily. They stopped at a table in a quiet corner by a window with a view of the mountainside, the ski slopes all lit up. "A special table with a special view."

"Oh, wow... Mari, *look*!" Bekka's expression was pure awe.

"Very cool. Although I can't imagine skiing at night. I can barely manage the daytime."

Another server came by with champagne and put it on ice on a stand next to the table, and yet another with two glasses of water.

"Fancy! I've had more champagne in the last few days..."

"I guess we're celebrating." Marissa took her hand and held her gaze. "Celebrating what though?"

"That we've reconnected. That you were brave enough to come here after the shit that went down."

Marissa nodded. "I'm glad we reconnected. I really am. But I don't know if it was brave. I needed out of New York."

"It was brave. You could have just been still. Entropy, you know?"

"I guess so. Maybe you're right. I can be pretty badass when I want to be." Mari shook her head and picked up her menu.

"You so can." Beks studied the menu for a minute. "Oh, do I want the steak or the risotto?"

"Risotto with a side of steak?" Mari waggled her eyebrows. "This all looks amazing, but tomorrow I want a big fat cheeseburger."

"Ooh... You know my thoughts about a bacon cheeseburger. Can we have onion rings too?"

"Of course, they're a must." Mari put her menu down. "Tonight I'm having the penne vodka."

"Mmm... I'm going for the risotto, I think, and a Caesar salad." Beks shook her head, grinned. "So, are you staying all the way through the holidays?"

"This honeymoon thing includes a Christmas dinner and pictures with Santa so hell yes I'm staying through Christmas. And then...we'll see. The brochure said First Night here is a big deal too, so...maybe I'll just stick around." Marissa poured them each a glass of champagne, then caught her eye. "You?"

"I'm staying, for sure. I love it here. It snows!"

"You're too much, pretty. We can't stay in the honeymoon suite forever."

"So, we'll get ourselves another room, or we could rent a place that's got a kitchen."

"I like that idea. Shack up for a week or two?" Mari winked at her. "I've just been so surprised by you."

"It's been new, that's for sure. I thought you hated me, but I don't think you do." Beks explored her face with a smile. "I think we were both in different places in our lives."

"You can say it. I took myself way too seriously. I tried too hard to be perfect. I know. I still like the ideal, but I'm just more realistic now."

"Me too." She caught Marissa with an arch look. "I am! I'm just not as grounded in the physical as you are."

Marissa huffed a laugh. "That makes me sound so shallow."

"I was thinking it made me sound so flighty..."

"Hm. Well, if I'm shallow, and you're flighty then we're meeting somewhere in the middle, right?" Marissa lifted her glass of champagne. "To the middle."

"To the middle." Beks waggled her eyebrows, so dirty. "I like your middle."

"Thank you. It's work, but I'm just shallow enough to be proud of it." Mari tried to keep a straight face, but she lost the battle.

"It's beautiful. I admit, though, I'm trying to love my curves."

"It's not so hard. I'm pretty fond of them."

Beks wiggled in her seat, and Marissa wanted to cheer. She'd done that, and Beks wasn't holding back at all.

God, she hoped she was doing the right thing, and this wasn't just a rebound relationship. She didn't want to hurt Bekka—if they were just fooling around that was one thing, but it felt like more than that. She was sure Bekka saw it as more than that.

She was sad, but didn't feel heartbroken anymore; she'd left all of that in New York. But did that mean she was ready for this? Was there any such thing? Maybe not.

Maybe she just needed to enjoy it, right now, and let herself relax for a minute. That was probably the most fair thing for Beks too.

"If I stick around after Christmas I'll have to work some...that okay?"

"Oh, I'm not independently wealthy. I'll have to take clients myself."

That made her smile. Someone who understood she had to work. She made good money, and it would go a lot farther outside of New York, but for now she still had rent to pay. "Great. Do you do a lot of virtual work?"

"One hundred percent. One of the reasons I can charge what I do is that I can make appointments at odd hours, that I can be there at midnight if I'm needed." Beks grinned, the expression a bit wry. "I know it's a niche need I'm filling, but my clients are good people, professionals and artisans who are needing support."

"You sound like a therapist. A fancy in-the-box therapist instead of a card reader."

"I am."

She nodded. "That wasn't meant to be insulting, I'm sorry. I just... I guess I need to see you in action, that's all. You know how I am." She was a skeptic. She believed in what she could see, hear, smell, taste--solid proof was her way of life.

"No, I mean, I'm a licensed counselor. I'm qualified to prescribe drugs in Texas. I just choose to communicate with my clients using the tarot."

She blinked and set her glass down. "You are? I'm so sorry, I had no idea. That's fantastic." And pretty much the perfect career for Bekka, who had always been as empathetic as they came.

"Thank you. I love my clients, and they are special people." Bekka beamed, and it was a good look on her, to be honest.

Lesson learned. Don't underestimate Bekka. And ask more questions.

This wasn't a competition. This was a...was journey too overused? It probably was. Didn't make it less true though.

The server took their orders and she leaned back in her chair, settling in, determined to get to know Bekka—*this* Bekka, not the one in her memory, but the version sipping champagne and looking so beautiful—much better.

10

"I'm waiting to hear about that rental downtown, Mari. It's an old Victorian, and so cute." There were stairs, but it was worth the hassle for the sheer adorable factor.

They had three more days at the hotel, and she was hunting for a space for another week, at least.

"All I need is Wi-Fi. But if it's cute, that's a nice bonus." Mari sipped her coffee and looked out the window. "It won't have this view, but downtown would be cool. In the middle of everything. I called my cat sitter; she's good for as long as I need her."

"What's your cat's name?" She did love Mari's butt. It was so sweet and squeezable.

"Poe. He's a black Maine Coon. He's a big dork and my best buddy." Mari wandered back over and pulled out her phone to show off a picture. "Isn't he pretty? He knows it too."

"Oh, so pretty! I just lost my girl—Wacky. She got cancer." And it had hurt, bone-deep, but that was how life happened.

"Wacky." Mari smiled gently. "I'm sorry she was sick. That's a great name. But you like cats?"

"Are you kidding? I love cats. My apartment only allows one, and I haven't been ready to find a new soul buddy."

"I hear that." Mari touched her cheek. "Okay, you. Are we getting out of here today?"

"Totally. I am at your disposal, and they say more snow is happening tomorrow, but today is supposed to be beautiful." And sunny. And sparkly. And—"This place is so pretty, Mari!"

"So outdoors first then. How about the gondola ride? I think we can get a shuttle over there."

"Ooh...can I do it with the cast? I'd love to take pictures." She could put them up on her Insta. It would be charming.

"I don't see why not. You can sit the whole time. It's one of the zillion things we have free tickets for."

"Then we need to go. I want to do everything with you." She wanted to experience and enjoy and any other 'e' words she could think of.

"All right then. Let's get going." Mari went and got her crutches, then helped her up.

She was beginning to get good at this, this whole crutching around without feeling like a dancing bear.

"I never asked you how long you'd be in that cast." Mari got the door for her and held it. "Does it still hurt?"

"Four weeks, and then a boot. Yay boot!" She winked at Mari and clumped out the door. "And no. It really doesn't. Cool, huh?"

"At least that's something." Mari closed the door behind them. "Pictures here we come. I hear you can see the valley and the village from up there."

"I'm excited." She loved this whole thing—well, not the

crutching part. That sucked. But the going and doing, the seeing new things, that was wonderful.

Being with Mari was too.

She hadn't realized how much she'd missed Marissa until she'd been able to reconnect.

The shuttle drivers all knew them by now; they were kind of a celebrity couple getting free rides and free adventures all week. And everyone believed they were married.

"Have a fantastic day, ladies!" the driver said as they exited the shuttle.

Slowly.

The driver watched as Mari helped her. So awkward. "And...bye!" the driver said again once she was actually off the shuttle.

Mari just giggled at her.

Bekka wasn't sure she'd ever heard Mari make that sound sober. It was cute as hell, and Bekka wanted to hear it again.

"Even the shuttle is an adventure, huh? But, nothing like door-to-door service."

"Well, you know, if that tree hadn't jumped in front of me, hmm?" Bekka's cheeks burned, but she made herself laugh, because she was the reason they were...galumphing along.

"Fucking tree." Mari deadpanned.

"Yep. It hates me. I'm not going to be a skier, I guess." She hadn't tried too hard, but once had been enough for right now.

"This is not the end of the world. Besides, it's good for couples to have some different hobbies." Mari blushed. It mixed in with the pink from the cold air, but it was unmistakably a blush. "You know...friend-couples. Who are mostly friends but kind of a couple. Sort of together, you know what I mean."

"I totally do. Fake-married couple-types." She wasn't going to walk away from this. No way. Mari could walk away.

"Right. Exactly." Mari looked at her. "Well, wait. No. More than fake-married-couple-types. Just not quite... definable. Yet."

"Fair enough. At least having fun together types, hmm?" She wanted that.

"Yes. That at the very least."

"Ready, ladies? Looks like you're getting a private ride." The gondola was small, meant to seat maybe eight people, but there was no one else in line.

"Oh, it's like it was meant to be..." Bekka carefully crutched into the tram, trying to be super careful. One fall was an accident. Two was clumsiness.

"Wait, I'll help." Mari was right at her side and assisted her in, then climbed in with her and helped her get seated. There was no clumsy fumbling of her crutches or awkward where should she put her hands moments, Mari just made it happen.

"Wow."

Mari blinked at her. "Wow, what?"

"You just—you make things easier." Maybe that was silly, but true was true.

"Thanks, I'd like to take credit, but everything is easier with two people, pretty." Mari sat next to her while the staff tucked the crutches into a little net by the door.

"Maybe." But she knew better. It wasn't more people. It was Mari.

"Okay, lovebirds. It's a beautiful clear day. Make sure you look down and find downtown Summit Springs. Have fun!"

The staff closed the doors and after a little lurch, they were moving.

"Oh... Oh, my god, Mari!" She grabbed Marissa's hand and held on, her heart racing with the sudden height.

Marissa laughed and put an arm around her. "You're not afraid of heights are you?"

"Of course not!" Goddess, this was high. Like really high. She held onto Mari's hand, though, even if she wasn't scared.

"Good." Mari held on too, leaning close. "It's so beautiful. Look at the view...the snow is sparkling."

"It's like a carpet of diamonds." And she felt like that was a good omen, like the Ten of Pentacles in the future.

Mari kissed her cheek. "We're lucky to get all of this special treatment. When I agreed to come out alone, I thought that would be it. Alone."

"I'm glad it wasn't." Bekka couldn't believe that someone wanted to hurt Mari, but she was also glad that she had this chance to try again.

She was tickled that Mari had filled out the entry form, which seemed so unlike her lover.

Fate.

The tram swayed, and she held on tight.

"Windy up here, huh? Look, you can see people skiing. They're so tiny."

"Uh-huh." Windy? More like gusty. Big gusty. Huge. "They make it look so easy."

"It's not easy and you need to stop—"

The gondola lurched just after it rolled over a support tower and they halted abruptly, literally swinging in the wind.

"Mari!" Her heart stopped. It just stopped. This wasn't going to work for her. At all.

Marissa squeezed her hand tight. "No worries. These things stop all the time. They're probably loading the next —"

They started to move and then jerked to stillness abruptly again.

"It's fine. Totally normal." Mari's voice was calm but that grip on her hands hadn't let up.

"Y-yeah? You think?" She wasn't sure she could even fake calm. Not right now.

"I'm sure this happens a lot. We'll just sit tight and breathe. It'll start up again in a minute."

A voice came through a speaker in the wall of the gondola car, but it was staticky and broken up. "Interruption in service...wind...engineers are restoring...back shortly."

Mari snorted. "God, that's almost worse than the subway speakers."

Bekka felt her stomach drop through her body and slam on the floor. She forced out a whispered. "Are we going to be stuck up here?"

"No." Mari turned to her and looked at her hard, right into her eyes. "No, we're not going to be stuck. It's okay. It's scary right now, but we're fine. We're going to be fine."

"Right." She was fine. Mari was fine. They were fine. "We're so having shots after this."

"Yes. Several. God, I wish I had some weed." Mari peered up at the sky. "So...who do you...like, who's your higher power? Maybe put in a good word? That might make you feel better."

"I have a lot of higher powers, but weed is legal here, so shots and edibles?"

"It's a date. As soon as we're back on solid ground. And the next time we decide to be adventurous, I'm going to let you do a reading first." Mari winked at her.

"Uh-huh. I thought it would be...not so high."

Mari nodded and pulled Bekka into her arms. "I didn't think it would be this windy. It's not as cold as it could be I guess. Are these things heated?"

"I think so." Mari was trembling, and that made her feel braver. "Kiss me?"

"What a great idea." Mari didn't hesitate and her kiss wasn't timid at all.

Oh, hell yes. She scooted closer, the danger and adrenaline making her shiver. This was possibly the most dangerous thing she'd ever done.

Mari's fingers slid up her thigh, tongue circling hers and the kiss grew deeper.

She reached for the bottom of Mari's sweater, searching for skin, for the warm, soft belly.

Mari opened her coat to give her better access and that hand pushed between her thighs.

Were they really doing this? Her fingertips found skin as Mari cupped her through her yoga pants. Oh, hell yes they were.

"Better be quick, this thing might start moving again," Mari whispered and arched against her fingers.

"Uh-huh." She popped the button on Mari's jeans. "First one to come buys the shots."

"Fuck. That's always me." Mari grinned against her lips, finger starting to rub and glide in just the right way through her leggings.

"Uh-huh..." Bekka wasn't sure what she was agreeing to, but she didn't really care. The lightning shooting up her spine? The silk of Mari's panties? The scent of Mari's need? She cared about those.

Mari rocked against her fingers with a moan and kissed her again. Those fingers found a rhythm and it seemed like Mari didn't care much about anything but Bekka.

Mari was soaking wet, and Bekka whimpered, so fucking turned on it hurt.

"Fuck. This is...fucking crazy and that feels so good." Mari wrestled her fingers under the elastic of her leggings. "Yeah, pretty. I feel you."

"Uh-huh. Hurry. This is better than being high." She began to nudge Mari's clit, rubbing in circles.

"We are high. Up." The little gondola car filled with their sounds, rocking a little more than it already was.

"Uh-huh. Don't stop. Please, love." She was more than willing to beg.

Mari was breathing heavily and rocking into her hand, completely unashamed to go after what she needed. "There. There! Oh god."

Hell yes. She pushed even closer, rubbing with all she had. Mari's fingers dug into her arm, and by now she knew what that little grimace on her lover's face meant.

"Yes. Yes! Oh fuck." Mari's eyes squeezed shut and then popped open and she shook, hips slowing, breathing hard, "Fuck, yes."

"Mmm...so pretty." She slowed her touch, drawing out the aftershocks.

"Shots on me," Mari whispered to her, and swirled determined fingers over her clit.

"On..." Oh, fuck her. Her eyes rolled and she bore down, demanding more.

"Yeah. Feel good? Come on, Beks." Mari gave her what she needed, speaking low and sexy.

"Feels like magic." The tight spring in her belly clenched, and she grabbed hold of Mari's arms.

Mari didn't let up, fingers keeping the rhythm just how

she needed it. "You're so beautiful. I can't keep my hands off you. I want to feel you come, pretty."

"Soon...oh fuck. Mari! Mari, please!" She arched, damn near tumbling down as she fell apart.

Mari caught her and kissed her, stealing her air.

All she could do was shiver, moaning into her lover's lips. "Love..."

"Beks, I—"

There was a loud hum and then the gondola started moving again, startling them both.

"Shit. Wow. Okay." Mari pulled away and started putting herself back together, tucking in her shirt and zipping her fly.

"Good timing." Bekka made sure she was okay, telling herself that she'd almost fucked up bad right then. Mari wasn't into more than a nice holiday fuck. She knew this.

She just didn't believe it.

"I don't know. I was enjoying myself." Mari looked around, then put an arm around her. "We're almost at the top, then we'll ride back down. Are you okay?"

"I'm melted, so yeah." Heights? Who cared?

"You're a sexy thing, Ms. Harker." Mari pulled her closer so she was almost in Mari's lap.

"You make me dizzy, Mari." It was like that perfect reading, when everything came together as if the stars had it planned.

"Better me than the heights, right?" Mari looked around suddenly, not out the windows, but inside the gondola car. "You don't think they have cameras in here do you?"

11

Oh, they'd had shots.

Many shots. They'd made some bar friends, ordered some food, then wandered around town for a while drinking coffee. Somehow they'd made it back to resort in an Uber or something that Marissa didn't think either of them had paid for.

She had no idea what time that was either, but they'd fooled around for a while and after they'd both gotten off, they'd crashed.

It had been a fun night. Late, but fun.

There was light streaming in the window, and she hid from it, burying her nose between Bekka's shoulder blades.

"Mmm... Morning, you." Bekka giggled softly. "Did we really sing 'Total Eclipse of the Heart' in the bar?"

"Morning. We would never do anything so humiliating." They totally had. "I think I did actually lick salt off your neck though."

Mmm. Tequila.

"Oh, yeah. That was hot as hell." Soft giggles filled the

air. "Not as hot as what I got to lick when we got back to bed."

She hummed, stretching out long. "And I thought you were uninhibited when you were sober. I had no idea what a couple of shots could do."

"Mmm...lime-flavored Mari. My new favorite taste." Bekka stretched and wiggled, so warm and silky against her.

"I don't do that very often, you know. Drink like that. Yesterday was something else." She knew damn well why too, and it had almost nothing to do with the gondola stalling halfway up the mountain.

"This is a special situation, Mari. We have so many things to feel, right?"

She didn't know if Bekka was a mind reader also, but sometimes it felt that way. She nodded. "It's a lot." She frowned after she said that and rolled up on an elbow to look at Bekka. "Good things. But a lot."

"Positive stressors are still stress." Beks shrugged and smiled at her. "You are allowed to give yourself time to process."

She laughed. "Uh-huh. It's definitely easier to give myself tequila instead and not have to process."

"You're on vacation another couple of days. Tequila is on the table." Bekka winked at her, teasing. "And on me. On your fingers."

She laughed, but Bekka had opened a door yesterday, and she didn't know what to do. Love was a very big word right now. The only thing she knew for sure was she didn't want Bekka to get hurt. "You might be better on crutches drunk. We should go back down there tonight."

"Works for me. I don't have any clients for another two days." Bekka's dark hair framed her face, like a thunderstorm before it broke.

"I haven't even checked my email once." *Since we started...this.* That seemed like a relevant detail. Something she should probably say out loud but didn't have the courage.

Oh, but did Bekka should check hers?

"Did we get the Victorian?"

"Yep. We have to run down and pick up the keys tomorrow. I signed the rental agreement when you were in the bathroom." Beks grinned at her. "Hopefully I spelled my name right."

"Hopefully?" She started laughing. "I'll Venmo you the rent. I can't believe we're staying." It might be nice. Working a little, just hanging out. "We can go to all the little restaurants, or cook in, walk to the coffee place in the morning..."

"I love the croissants there. I'm going to have to crutch everywhere so I can fit in my jeans." Beks rolled up and stretched tall. All those pretty curves were displayed to perfection, from the roll of her hip to the way her pretty full breasts were crowned with pink nipples hardened in the cool air.

Mari reached out and ran her fingers down the side of one perfect breast. "So pretty." Beks was the best cure for her hangover.

Oh, that nipple just tightened for her.

"You say the nicest things, Mari. You make me want to sing."

She sat up, slipped an arm around Beks. "I just want you to know. I'm in a weird place but I appreciate you. I'm really enjoying this."

"Good." Beks caught her gaze. "You don't have to say that you love me, you know? You aren't going to hurt my feelings.

It's only been a couple of days. I've been in love with you forever, and I'm impulsive. You are in the clear."

"Forever?" Beks was so honest. She wasn't even sure she wanted to be in the clear.

"Yeah. I mean, don't get me wrong, I've had amazing lovers. I've had affairs and relationships, but you're my one that got away."

"Me? I was kind of awful." Maybe not specifically to Beks but just generally young and stupid. She definitely hadn't appreciated Bekka's spirit.

"You were driven, and I was scared and flighty. I had a ton of therapy, and I had to accept that you might never like the person that I was becoming." Beks shrugged, but the motion didn't read defensive somehow. "And I may never have liked the person you wanted to become. But I do."

"I do too. The second I saw you again I assumed I wouldn't, but I was wrong." Beks wasn't scared or flighty. She was creative and insightful. She was free spirited and honest.

"Thank you." That smile—open and loving and beautiful?—that was worth a fortune. She'd never seen anything so fine.

She caught Bekka's chin with one finger and turned her head for a short kiss. "What should we do today?"

"Don't we have a—"

Marissa's phone started ringing, "Bitch" by Meredith Brooks sounding. Damn. The ex.

She ignored it. Whatever that was about could wait, she was in bed with her new girlfriend. Her new, hot girlfriend, thank you very much. Her new, hot, not cheating on her girlfriend.

The bitch in question could leave a voicemail.

"Mmm..." Beks reached over and killed the sound. "Love

that song, but it's not on our list, hmm?"

"Nope. That's just someone I used to know. I can't even imagine what she could want."

Beks shot her an evil fucking grin. "I bet I can."

"What? Apologize? Ask me to come back? Booty call?" She shook her head. "Please. She would never. She's a coward."

"And a moron. Luckily for you, I am neither, right?"

"You are brave and beautiful, way more fun, and smarter than I am."

Beks blinked at her. "I—Thanks. Seriously."

She took Bekka's hand and kissed it. "So what were you saying we're supposed to do today?"

Her phone started to ring again, the sound making them both jump.

"Ugh. Hand it to me?" Beks handed her the phone and Marissa answered it. "Hello?"

"Marissa! You haven't answered my texts! I've been worried!"

Worried? Seriously? Josie had actually been texting her several times a day. They were incoherent and useless, and she'd deleted them all as they'd come in. She looked at Beks and shrugged. "I'm not answering your texts because you dumped me, Josie."

"I had a change of heart. You wowed me, with all that you did to keep me."

Oh, bullshit.

"I'm sorry, Josie, I've moved on. I'm also not that stupid." She needed to hang up. This was not a conversation she wanted to have.

"Moved on? Moved *on*?"

Wait. Was she hearing Josie's voice in her phone and in the hallway? Was that possible?

"How do you move on from I want to marry you?"

She frowned at Beks and mouthed, "Is she here?"

Beks nodded, slowly pointing at the suite door.

What the actual fuck? She slipped out of bed to find her robe. "You cheated on me and told me you were in love with someone else. That kind of makes the heart grow cold, Josie."

"Not to mention the basic creep factor," Beks whispered, snagging a pair of sweatpants.

"So creepy," she mouthed back, tying her robe. "I'm hanging up, Josie."

"I want to make things up to you, baby."

She hung up the phone, debating whether to open the suite door.

Bekka bit her bottom lip, holding in the giggles. "I'm going to call my brother."

"Reinforcements. That's a great idea." How did Josie even know what room they were in? "I think you should go home, Josie," she called through the door.

"Can't we just talk? Have a drink? One drink?"

"It's...oh." Okay, looking at the clock, she was surprised to find it was much later in the day than she thought it was, but still a little early for a drink. "There's really nothing to talk about."

This was bad though. Not just because it was insane for Josie to show up, but it was making her feel...bad. Angry. Upset. How dare Josie just show up here?

"Go home, Josie. Just go."

"No. I love you, and I want to do it. I want to marry you. You loved me enough to ask me, didn't you?"

Beks moved toward the unused second bedroom, eyes wide.

That was enough. She didn't want a scene in the hallway.

She went to the door and tugged it open. "Get in here." She stepped out of the way so Josie could come inside and closed the door behind her. "Have you lost your mind?"

"Have you? This was going to be our honeymoon! It still could be."

"You cheated on me." That was the simple fact. "You were with someone else. You didn't want me."

And there was someone next door that did.

"I was just...sowing my wild oats." Josie came sauntering up. "Come on, baby. You know how hot we are together."

"Were." Fuck. This was the Josie she'd fallen for, all this swagger and heat. "I'm not interested anymore, Josie. And you can't just show up in my life like this anymore."

"I did, though, and I'm going to make it up to you." Josie moved closer, then her eyes narrowed. "You've got a hickey. You naughty girl. You were cheating too."

"No." She took a step back, trying to put some space between them. "Who I've been with or not with since you dumped me is none of your business. But I wasn't with anyone before but you." She didn't need to justify herself to Josie.

A knock came to the hotel room door. "Ms. Martin? Do you need assistance?"

Ah, Bryan.

"Hello, Bryan. Yes, please." She moved around Josie in a wide arc to get the door.

"I'm sorry for the inconvenience. Ma'am, you'll need to come with me." Bryan looked at Josie as he entered the room, then motioned behind him at the door.

"What? No! I'm the wife! I belong here."

"Ma'am, I will call the police and have you arrested for trespassing. Please, come with me." Look at Bryan, being all businesslike and forceful.

Now that she had a little distance, she could breathe again. "Goodbye, Josie. You cheating little twat."

"Don't say I didn't give you another chance, baby. You want to end things? This is your fault." Bryan was herding Josie from the room, but she kept on talking.

"I take full fucking credit! Thank you, Bryan." Marissa slammed the door feeling powerful for all of two seconds, and then she burst into tears.

"Oh, Mari..." Suddenly Beks was right there, arms soft and warm around her. "I have you."

"I'm so sorry." She leaned for a second, then remembered Bekka's foot and looked at her, sniffling. "You need to sit. We should sit."

"I'm all about sitting." Bekka used her sleeve to dab at her tears. "You're amazing."

She snorted and shook her head as she helped Beks get to the little couch at the end of their suite. There was a stool there that Beks liked to put her foot up on.

"She actually accused *me* of cheating." She swiped at her eyes, wishing the tears would stop.

"Right? I don't understand what she was thinking. You're not a fool." Bekka never stopped touching her.

"She probably *was* thinking I'm a fool. I was before. I didn't see what was going on, I let her get away with everything." She was a complete idiot.

"Not today you didn't."

She nodded, studying her fingers. "No." That was true; she'd gotten to put Josie in her place. "I was mad today. Who does that? She's impulsive, but to fly all the way out here? That was just...bizarre."

"You must have a thing for women that follow their hearts, huh?" Bekka chuckled, soft and sweet, but a little sad.

"Yeah. I think I do." Josie wasn't following her heart

though, she was following her ego. But she knew Beks meant what she was saying. She was struck suddenly by the image of Beks shrinking away into the next room. "God, I'm so sorry to do that to you. Are you okay?"

"I'm solid. I just wanted to give you space, and to call Bry and have him come up." Bekka squeezed her hand, holding on.

"Thanks for doing that. He was awesome. I'm glad you're here." She kissed Bekka's fingers. It was nice to have someone make her a priority. She liked how that felt.

"I'm proud I didn't pop her in the nose. Oh. Or kick her in the shins."

"I would totally have backed you up if you had. I'm more of a scratch your eyes out type." She laughed but it came out more bitter than she'd intended.

"You were strong, firm, and I was proud of you. She was gaslighting you in the worst way, and I'd say that if I wasn't interested in being with you."

"She...does that. And thank you." She glanced at Beks. "I think I'm over that bitch."

"Good. I think you're amazing, and I want to kick her butt."

"No." She appreciated the sentiment though. She rubbed at her eyes, which had finally stopped leaking all over. "You want to forget she ever existed and kiss me."

"Who existed?" Bekka leaned right in, kissing her like she was delicate, precious.

Nobody.

She returned the kiss and it felt as if Beks was new, like she'd just learned something she didn't know yesterday. She didn't know she'd needed someone in her corner so badly.

And it felt like Bekka was. She didn't feel like Bekka had

been jealous of Josie, or worried, but she'd been respectful instead of *Marissa*.

She needed to step up. That's how she felt. Like Beks a made her want to be...better. She'd never been with anyone that inspired her that way. Maybe she hadn't given Beks the chance the first time around.

Maybe they hadn't been ready.

Maybe it just hadn't been the right time and place.

Bekka would love that idea.

She leaned in, pushing Beks back into the couch cushions.

"Mmm...yummy." Beks nipped her bottom lip, teasing the hell out of her.

She cupped Bekka's ass, one of her legs slipping in between when there was a knock on the door.

"Bekka? Marissa? Are y'all all right?"

"Goddamn it, Bry," Beks groaned, shaking her head. "When do we move to the house again?"

She laughed and pushed off the couch, giving Beks another quick peck. "Be nice; he was just my knight in shining armor." She opened the door. "We're fine, come in. I'm so sorry about all of that. Thank you so much."

"I'm so sorry. I assume she figured out you had to be in the upper floors and thought she'd hear you?"

"It's not your fault. She's..." Marissa waved it off. "I'm just glad I didn't marry her. And that she didn't try to punch you or something."

"I'd just have yelled for Bekka. She's a stud." Bryan winked at her, his eyebrows gyrating.

She turned to look at Beks, who had her foot up and her arms crossed. "She is pretty badass. I mean, look at how she fought off that tree and got away!"

Beks gasped, lips forming an 'O'. "Oh...oh, that was so

mean!"

Bryan though, he was laughing his ass off.

She grinned and went back to Beks on the couch. "Your superpowers are all in here." She tapped Bekka's chest. "You don't even need a phone booth."

"You just wanted to touch my boob, Mari."

"Ew! *Girls!*"

She laughed. "This is my honeymoon after all."

"Oh, right. I'd almost forgot. Happy Christmas Eve. Did you guys want to do anything this afternoon? The world will be closed down by six p.m."

"Beks had something but she's been interrupted twice... what have you been trying to tell me we're supposed to do, pretty?"

"Well, we have the sleigh ride, but maybe we should do that after Christmas and give the driver Christmas Eve off?"

"She's going to work whether you're the ones in her sleigh or not. Take the ride, and then I'll get you some reservations in town for a nice dinner for your last night here."

"It's not our last night. Your sister rented us a house in town through New Year's." A week didn't seem long enough anymore, but that was a bridge to cross later.

"Really? So we can have Christmas dinner!" Bryan grinned broadly.

"Is that cool with you, Mari? A nice holiday supper with Bry?"

It really didn't matter because no one was going to have to cook or clean up. Well, someone was, but they'd be earning time and a half for it.

"I would love that. I really would." That was the right thing to say about a holiday dinner with family, but she was half surprised to discover that she actually meant it too.

"Cool. We're having a limited menu, but it should be tasty—ham or roast, potatoes, rolls, green beans, and pies."

"That works. Better than peanut butter sandwiches, right, Bry?"

Beks got a knowing grin. "Hell, yeah."

"This sounds like a good story to hear over dinner." She stood again. "Sign us up for that sleigh ride. We'll be there with bells on."

"Perfect. I'll call Evie and let her know. I've had your... problem removed from the property, so she shouldn't be back."

"You are the best, Bryan. Thank you so much." She saw Bryan out and closed the door. "I thought he was delusional for a while, but he's a good guy."

"He really is. He tries so hard to make everyone happy that it gets him in trouble sometimes." Beks shrugged, twining their fingers together. "He's a great brother."

"We're going on a sleigh ride." She was excited. It sounded like fun. And kind of...romantic? "Another thing I've never done."

"Me either. I think I need go into town and pick up a present for Bry. Do you want to?"

"Yes. I do. It's so cute there right now with all the holiday decorations." Plus they had bar friends they might run into.

"Yeah, and we can stop and see if that bartender survived the night."

She chuckled. "I feel like we're not the first drunk, lesbian tourists she's dealt with, but then again she's probably never heard us sing before."

She helped Beks off the couch. "Let's get showered and dressed. I want to wash that bitch out of my hair."

Beks laughter chased her, all the way into the bathroom.

Her lady approved.

12

B ekka was proud of herself.

She hadn't had a meltdown when Mari's ex had shown up. She hadn't cried. She hadn't been a little bitch.

She'd wanted to, though, and she'd taken a long minute to look at her cards.

She dropped the ten of cups three different times as she shuffled, and that had calmed her heart.

Harmony. Alignment. Divine love.

Oh, maybe she'd done the right thing.

She pulled on a warm pair of fuzzy leggings and a bright green sweater. She wanted to buy Mari a Christmas gift as well as Bry.

"I'm about ready; do you need any help?" Mari came in wearing jeans, tall boots and a purple cable-knit sweater. Her dark hair was down but pulled back in a barrette. "Oh, I love your sweater! What a great color."

"Thank you." She posed herself, all dramatic and wild. It did show off her curves really well, didn't it?

"We are going to spend money and have a nice lunch

before our sleigh ride. I need to send some presents to Poe and his cat sitter, and maybe some little things to my team."

"Oh, that would be sweet. I want to stop at that little curio shop on Main. It's got a great energy." And Bekka might find that right thing for Mari.

"Okay. And can we stop in the little art co-op place? I think I want to send that neat mirror I was looking at to Laney. That's my cat-sitter's name. She's about seventy-five going on fifty."

"Absolutely. I think that shop is amazing. I may pick a thing or two up for myself, you know?" Mari had been eyeing a gorgeous hand-woven shawl in blues and purples. Bekka could totally grab it.

"Well, yeah. I have never gone shopping and not bought something for myself." Mari helped her get her coat on. "I think I need a gondola ornament."

Bekka's cheeks started to heat, but she couldn't have stopped it for love or money.

Mari laughed and tugged her hat on. "You want one too, huh? Come on, pretty. Let's go shop."

"I'm in. Let's go." She grabbed her crutches, moving easier now, the heavy cast more maneuverable.

The resort was still rolling out the red carpet, and the shuttle was waiting for them when they got to the lobby. Mari helped her get in and settled and they were in town in no time.

"We picked a great day for this, huh? Sunny, not too cold..." Mari helped steady her as she got out of the van.

"I like the snow part, though. Have you ever driven in this sort of stuff?" She hadn't, but she thought she needed to learn.

"When I was younger and living at home I did, but I haven't in years. I don't even own a car. I guess it's good that the place you found us is within walking distance." Mari glanced at her cast. "Oh, maybe not really."

"I'll be fine. Maybe I'll get a sled to put on my foot..." That was a funny idea. Crutch, sliiiiide, crutch, sliiiide.

"I could pull you on one of those round plastic ones. They glide over anything." She got a wink. "Or, you know, Uber is a thing."

"Sledding sounds way more exhilarating, doesn't it?" They stopped to reset, because they were laughing so hard.

"It does, but the last thing you need is a run-in with a fire hydrant or something." Mari giggled all the way through that gem.

"Oh, I am going to kick your hot butt." That would be a challenge, but Bekka might get her knee up there...

"Yeah? Good luck with that." Mari wiggled said hot butt at her.

"Mmhmm." If she was in that wheelchair, she could get a double handful.

Mari turned around, still smiling and made sure she was steady. "Should we start at your curio place? It's right up here I think."

"Sounds good." She glanced over at Mari. "I'm glad we're here, together."

It seemed important to point out.

"I'm glad I'm with you, too." Summit Springs did a pretty good job of keeping the sidewalks clear of snow and ice, and they moved along easily. "I'm looking forward to sharing the house, relaxing a little, even if we have to work. It'll be nice."

"I agree. I had a positive card pull this morning after our *visitation*. It was great."

"Visitation. Haha." Mari laughed. "You're pulling cards about us now?"

"I always draw a card about my day. You just happen to be a big part of my day, honey." Like the biggest part.

"Oh. So that's like pulling a card about my day then too. Sort of? What does that do for you? To know what's coming?"

"It's a way to center. To get in touch with my wants and needs." She knew that it was a strange way of mediating or self-reflection, but it was effective. "Or to acknowledge my fears and concerns."

"I wish I had that kind of faith in cards. Or fate. Or whatever that is."

"I'm not sure it's faith in anything but my own self, my higher self." Bekka chuckled softly. "Tonight, I'll show you. Let you see that it's not hocus pocus, but focus and self-reflection."

Mari nodded. "Okay. I'm in. I can't say I don't understand and then not let you try to explain it, right?"

Well, Mari could, but the fact that she wasn't doing it made her feel ten thousand feet tall.

"This is the place, right?"

"It is. I want to find Bry something silly, maybe a puzzle or some such." He needed more play in his life. Seriously.

Mari was in a very good mood considering the morning they'd had. "Where is your family?"

"Momma passed away about three years ago—breast cancer—and Daddy is remarried to a lady in Sweden. He left for vacation and never came back." It had been great for him, and she had a new place to visit. Dallas was getting lonely, though.

"Wow. Do you see him? I've never been to Sweden; it seems like such a long trip."

"I have, yes. It's great. So beautiful. I've been twice, and it's amazing."

"I bet. Oh, puzzles. Look at these; they're like sculptures." Mari picked one up. "The Empire State Building. Cool."

"Oh, that's neat, isn't it? And there's the Taj Mahal!" Bry would love that, she thought. It would be a challenge, something beautiful.

"Very pretty. And different. And it would take him a while, which might be a good thing?" Mari picked up a smaller one that was a tiger and then another that was a perfectly round ball. "Hm. Something like this would work for my team too. I'll think about it."

"Bry's not a big art guy, so a puzzle would be better." She handed it to Mari, because she couldn't crutch and carry.

"Got it. Are we going to sing on our sleigh ride? Seems like we should. I can't believe tomorrow is Christmas already."

"You know it!" She loved to sing, even if she wasn't any good at it.

"We're all warmed up for it after our stellar karaoke performance." Mari chuckled. "Speaking of which, are you hungry? We should go get lunch after this."

"I could so eat—you want burgers? Sandwiches? Pizza?" Or soup. Soup sounded perfect. "Maybe a nice soup with a piece of bread."

"Ooh. Soup. Or stew. Or chili." Mari grabbed a couple of the smaller puzzles as they moved along.

"Yeah. That sounds great to me. Tomato soup in a bread bowl." She licked her lips and hummed.

Mari set the presents down on the counter, and the sales-clerk smiled at Bekka. "How sweet. She's you're hero, right? Carrying everything for you?"

"She was my hero before that. This just makes her a

stud, too." She did have a backpack to hold the things they needed.

"That's me. I just need a cape and a muscle shirt."

The clerk blinked at Mari who kept an absolutely straight face. "That's a look."

"Totally. The sequins make it." Bekka could keep a straight face with the best of them.

"A sparkly cape? I'm in." Mari's fingers threaded with hers and held on.

"Excellent. I love the visual." The shopkeeper winked at Bekka, making her chuckle.

"I don't share, but, trust me, I do too."

Mari laughed as they paid for their gifts, but Bekka noticed the blush anyway. Mari let her hand go so she could pack the backpack. Then helped her get it back on.

"You two have a Merry Christmas."

"Thanks. You too." Mari held the door. "Do you want me to carry that?"

"I'm good right now. I may before we're done. Art store or food next?" She was easy. This was heaven.

"Food. I'm hungry now that you suggested soup. By the time we get there you're going to be ready to sit anyway."

"Yeah." No shit on that. This was hard exercise. Way more challenging than the gym. "I think you're right."

"Whitewater Tavern. That place looks good." And it was right here. "That's...wait, is that bar we were at last night?"

"Uh-huh." At least she thought so. It was a little fuzzy.

"I thought it looked familiar. Well, they had a big menu, so...dare we?" Mari winked at her.

"I bet the daytime staff is totally different."

"Mari! Beks! Our singing duet of love!"

Oh goodness.

"Hi!" Mari smiled and waved, then leaned close to her and whispered, "Wait. I don't remember her name, do you?"

"Nope. We called her 'pretty tequila girl'." At least that was her recollection.

"Right. Shit." Mari took a few steps ahead of her and smiled at the woman. "No singing today. We're just hungry."

"Aww...that's a shame. We had fun last night, didn't we, ladies?"

A huge group cheered.

"More fun than we can really remember." Mari chuckled. "Right, pretty?"

"You know it, babe, but we were sore this morning, so it was fun." She winked over, teasing hard.

"Grab a booth, and I'll bring you some menus. What are you drinking?"

"Water," Mari answered quickly.

"I'll take a Diet Coke for now, thanks, honey." Bekka wasn't sure she was ever drinking again.

"When you're drinking, the first round is on me!" The grin she got was pure wicked, from a flannel-shirted buff woman holding a pretty lady on one arm, a leash in the hand. The leash led to a wagging hound dog that looked happy as a clam.

Mari's eyes lit up. "Puppy! May I?"

"Sure! He's a sweetheart. His name is Goober, and he loves attention." The woman winked at the pretty little thing in her arms. "These two were having a good time last night while I was in here with Evie. I'm Lars, by the way, and this here is my better half, Charlotte."

"Hi. I'm Marissa, this is—uh..." Mari actually glanced at her. "Sorry. This is my *girlfriend*, Rebekka." Marissa shook their hands quickly, then bent to play with Goober, who was all lolling tongue and love. "Oh, you are the best aren't you?"

Goober licked her, butt wiggling, tail going ninety to nothing.

"Good boy. I love that they allow dogs in here." Mari stood up again and hooked an arm around her, letting her lean. "Beks needs to sit down. Are you just walking in? Did you want to join us for lunch?"

Lars glanced at Charlotte, who smiled and nodded. It worked for Bekka, barring the whole struck-dumb-by-the-girlfriend thing.

She did manage a smile and a nod.

"Good, come sit. We're still not drinking yet, though. We overdid it a little last night. Are you okay in a booth, Beks? Or there's a table right there."

"I'm cool in a booth. Less ways to bump into me. Last night was a hoot, wasn't it?" They headed over and sat, stashing her crutches and settling.

Then, once they were seated, she reached for Mari's hand. Mari pulled her hand over to rest on Mari's thigh and tangled their fingers.

"What happened last night?" Charlotte asked as if she knew how drunk they'd been and opened her menu.

Mari leaned back in her seat. "Before or after we almost died on the gondola ride?"

"Oh, that thing?" Charlotte snorted. "Someone should have warned you. How many times does that get stuck in a week, Lars? Six? Ten? Every time the wind blows?"

"Lots, but it's a nice excuse to make out and chill." Lars gave Charlotte a long, slow look that said without a doubt that they hadn't been the first girls to get off in that gondola.

Mari laughed. "Oh, for sure. So after we chilled on the gondola, we ended up here for shots."

Bekka snorted. "And did we ever have a few."

They hadn't slammed them, though. It had been a long, slow drunk—ending in happy, sloppy lovemaking.

"Oh, we've been there. Did I hear something about karaoke?"

Mari groaned. "Unfortunately?"

"Stop. You were great. It was so much fun." Pretty Tequila Girl set waters down for them. "Hungry?"

"Yes, please." Mari finally opened her menu. "I'm sorry. I don't mean to be rude, but what was your name again?"

The woman laughed. "Katharine. And don't worry, you met like fifteen of us last night, you're not going to remember our names, even if you were sober."

"We'll get them figured out, don't you worry." Because this wasn't going to be the last time they were in this bar. She believed that.

"Most of us came here from out of town, we get it." Katharine took their order—soup and chili for them, Lars and Charlotte were splitting some kind of hot sandwich. "Let me know when you're switching to beer," Katharine teased, winking as she headed back toward the bar.

Charlotte picked up her Coke. "So, you just moved here? You two look so good together."

"No. We're staying at the lodge—my brother works there. We've got a house we're renting downtown for the next two weeks," Bekka said.

"Spending Christmas here? Let us know if you need a tree. Lars has a farm."

"A tree farm?" Mari sounded interested. "How cool."

"Yeah, and I'm giving the cut ones away today. They need homes."

Charlotte rolled her eyes. "Lars is about to make me a Dog Sled Widow."

"A what?" Those words didn't make sense.

"I'm a dog sledder." Lars snorted. "Charlotte is exaggerating...mostly."

"Mostly. When she's not trying to get eaten by a moose." Charlotte gave Lars a teasing smile.

"You dog sled? Wild. We're going on a sleigh ride later. We're looking forward to it." Mari gave her the most adoring look. "I assume that's horses though."

"Oh, yeah. That's Evie. She and Cheyenne run the ranch, a little bakery, and a guest house."

Summit Springs was a friendly sort of town, that was for sure.

"Neat. It feels like everyone knows everyone around here. I guess that's a good thing? I'm not used to it, I live in New York, we mostly know the people we work with or whatever. A few friends."

"Wow!" Lars's eyes went wide. "Do you go to the big parade and see the balloons?"

Mari laughed. "The Macy's parade? God, no. Too many people, too cold, too hard to get around. I watch it on TV."

"Oh, that's a bummer to hear. I've always wanted to go."

Bekka chuckled and nodded. "I went to the Rose Parade once in Pasadena. It was amazing." She'd stayed in an apartment with a friend, and they'd sat on the balcony and watched from above. The smell of all the flowers had been amazing.

"Pasadena is a little warmer." Mari winked at her.

"Yeah, yeah, and I bet having an apartment you can see it from is *pricey*!" But it was still a great thought—a giant balloon eye looking in at you.

"Definitely. No thank you."

"I can't imagine living in New York." Charlotte shook her head. "I moved to Denver for a while, but I was glad to come home. It wasn't what I thought it would be."

"So you're from here?"

"We both are."

"That's cool. I kind of thought it was mostly tourists."

"We are a tourist town, especially in the summers, but we have a thriving local situation." Charlotte's eyes lit up. "Fall festival, Christmas bazaar, Easter egg hunt, summer art show…"

Wow. Someone was very involved. Very.

"It's too bad we didn't know we were staying this long, we could have gotten Beks a booth at the bazaar. She reads tarot."

"Oh, that would have been so cool! I would love to have something like that down at the farm. Or even at the farmer's market."

"Well, you never know, do you?" Bekka thought she was going to stay. She thought she was going to hope that Mari stayed too.

Was that insane?

"Farmer's Market is a great idea. And I can get you into next year's bazaar, if you're around." Charlotte leaned back in her seat as their food arrived. "Oh, yum."

Everything smelled good, but best of all was the fact that no one stared when Lars fed Charlotte a French fry.

Mari dug into her chili. "Mm. Oh, this was a good idea, Beks."

"Right? I was craving something hot and wet."

She didn't think about what she'd said until she realized everyone was grinning at her.

"Well, shit. You could have just asked. It would have been cheaper than lunch." Mari leaned toward her.

Bekka leaned in as well, brushing their lips together. "Oh, honey—you've never been cheap. Not once."

Mari took that offer and kissed her, grinning. "Thank you. I think?"

"That's totally a compliment." Charlotte tossed her hair and wiggled, so dramatic. "It's perfect in fact."

"Mhm. Pretty damn perfect." Mari gave her a wink and went back to her chili.

People came and went—obviously everyone knew Lars and Charlotte, and they'd apparently made an impression last night as well. Everyone chatted a bit and moved on.

Bekka was in love.

"We better get moving, since we have a sled waiting for us. This has been really nice, though. Thanks for joining us."

"I'm practically the welcome committee." Charlotte beamed at them. "I'm sure we'll see you again since you're staying in town for a bit. Come get a tree if you want one. The leftovers are small, but they're are a few cute ones left."

"Thanks."

Mari grabbed her crutches, helping her as she wound her way through the crowded restaurant.

"That was nice, right? I sort felt like I belonged there."

"It was great. It—I think it's going to be impossible to go back to Dallas after seeing this place."

Mari glanced at her with an interested look on her face, but it disappeared quickly. "Well, your brother is here, so it's a natural move for you."

"My brother moves around. I tend not to, huh? What about you?" Bekka wanted to ask Mari to...what? Come and find a condo with her?

"Well, I thought I was a New Yorker. But I told you, New York is...*her* now. And after the insanity Josie just pulled I don't think I'm going to stay there long. And I can work here. These days, I can work anywhere."

"Yeah? That's where I am. And I want to see where this takes—" Us. "—things."

"This?" Mari gave her a knowing grin. "Things? I know what you're asking, Beks. And I know the answer. I'm just a little afraid of saying it out loud."

"Me too. It's crazy fast." And it was a little like the U-Haul joke made flesh, but it still felt right.

"I thought I was ready to marry someone else a month ago. This is... I can't believe I was so wrong about her. I can't believe you're here. I'm just stunned by all of it."

"So, let's just have a great day, a relaxing week, then we talk more. Fair?" She wasn't going back to Dallas to stay. Period.

Mari nodded. "More than fair." They stepped back into the cold weather but the sun was warm on their faces and she barely felt the chill.

13

The air was frosty, but Marissa was warm, tucked under a heavy blanket with her arms around Beks, who'd been snuggled in and leaning against her since the start of their sleigh ride.

Her nose was frozen but she'd never been more comfortable in her life.

Or happier.

Or felt more at home.

The sleigh zoomed along through the woods, and every so often the late afternoon sun would blind her for a second, or shine in Bekka's hair, turning it to gold for a moment.

"Over the river and through the woods," she sang in Bekka's ear, loud enough to be heard over the wind.

"This is... Oh, Mari. Thank you. This is magic!" Those pretty eyes were fastened on her, so wide, so happy.

She couldn't take any credit; this was one of those honeymoon freebies, but she didn't know if Beks was really talking about the sleigh ride. She honestly didn't know anything except that she wanted to do everything she could to keep the smile in those gorgeous eyes.

She smiled back and tugged Beks in tighter. "This is amazing. Aren't the horses amazing?"

"Beautiful. You can tell how well they're taken care of. They just shine." Beks grinned, shaking her head. "We're in a sleigh, Mari! Like a real-life sleigh."

"I don't think I've ever been in a sleigh. And I know I've never kissed a hot as fuck woman in a sleigh. You're the first." She caught Bekka's nape and kissed her, soaking in some of her joy.

"Mmm." Beks leaned in, one mittened hand landing on her thigh. "Merry Christmas, lover."

"Merry Christmas, love." The simplest answer was the truth, however preposterous.

"Yes. Love." Beks stole another kiss, sweet and slow and soft. "This is perfect. I always want snow at Christmas."

"I hate snow in New York. I love it here." She didn't mind the cold as much here either.

The sleigh slid along through a narrow path that opened up onto a wide open, snowy field and bright sunshine. Their driver turned slightly toward them. "The horses love to run here. Are you okay with that?"

"We're good! We're great," she shouted back, grinning as the sleigh took off at a good clip.

Bekka's delight was obvious, shining from her face, even as she clung to Marissa's hand.

"Woo hoo!" She held Bekka's hand, and shouted into the wind, enjoying the ride. "Feels safer than the gondola did, right? Way more fun."

"Well...the gondola got fun, Mari."

Wicked girl!

"It was memorable for sure." She stuck out her tongue. It was absolutely a top ten in her book.

"It was more than that, Mari. It was magical. I loved how you made me fly."

Bekka hadn't been the only one on cloud nine that afternoon.

The snow whizzed by as they went up and over a little hill and the whole valley opened up for them. "Look at this view." She loved this place. The more she saw, the more she fell in love with it. And with Bekka. She was completely taken with the idea of staying here, with Bekka and all of this.

"I want to be here, with you, next Christmas," Bekka stated.

She searched Bekka's eyes, as if they could confirm what she already knew, then nodded. "I'm thinking Valentine's Day, Easter, Fourth of July, Halloween and Thanksgiving too."

"Arbor Day, St. Patrick's, Labor Day. I'm in."

"When the hell is Arbor Day?" She laughed as the sled took a corner and sent them both sliding.

Beks was almost in her lap, curves pressing into her, soft and warm. Perfect.

Their driver turned around again as the sled slowed down. "I usually drop people off near town, but you'd have a little bit of a walk to get to Conifer Avenue. Would you rather I take you around to the ski lodge?"

She looked at Beks. "What do you think, pretty?"

"I think that would be perfect. Do you mind? It's a ride."

She got a wink and a tip of the white hat. "My lady's at the lodge. I'll pick her up there and bring her home."

This really was a woman's town.

"You want to do that reading for me when we get back? I guess we need to pack. Maybe I'll get one more dip in the hot tub." She needed to call Laney and see about getting Poe here and her apartment...

"Do you want to go back to New York with me?"

She blurted that out before she gave it real thought.

"Yes." Beks didn't even hesitate. "We can decide where to go together from there."

Just like that. Yes. We. Together.

"Are you sure? I kind of have to close things up there and figure out what to do with my apartment, get Poe...it's okay if you don't."

"Yes. My apartment will be fast, and the rent's not near like yours. You first, then decisions, then mine. Fair?"

She nodded, smiling at the idea of showing Beks the fun parts of New York. "Okay. Yeah. Thank you."

"Of course. I love you. It's a thing." Beks bounced on the seat, expression pure joy. "Merry Christmas Eve! I love you!"

"Merry Christmas Eve, Beks." She would never have Bekka's outward joy, but she felt it inside. "I love you too."

"Good. Good, we're going to be...we're going to have so much fun."

The sleigh stopped almost directly in front of the lodge, just across from it where everyone kept their skis. "This is it, ladies. I hope you had a great time."

"It was perfect, Evie. Thank you so much. It was absolutely the coolest."

The cowboy—cowgirl?—helped Beks out of the sleigh and got her settled on a bench before helping her out.

"Thank you so much. This was amazing. We really enjoyed it." She sat with Beks, holding her girl's crutches as the sled pulled away.

"So, that was amazing. I can't imagine a more perfect Christmas Eve."

"Oh, the night is young." Mari had a few things in mind

to make the night a little more special. "We still have naked-type things left to do. And maybe have some cocoa. Or just the whipped cream."

"Ooh...you do have the best ideas." Beks slipped one arm around her waist.

She figured she should get her hot little one-foot-wonder into the hotel before they tried to burn down the bench they were sitting on, plus a black car had just pulled up and she wasn't really interested in putting on a show.

"Marissa." Josie stepped out of the car.

Oh, Jesus Christ. Again? "You're supposed to be gone."

"I'm on my way to the airport. Can we have one minute alone please? Just a minute."

She glanced at Bekka. "I don't think so. Beks and I are—"

"Marissa." Josie actually grabbed her hand. "I want to apologize."

Okay. She was owed one, not that it would change anything. "Fine, go ahead."

"Alone."

Beks tilted her head, full lip curling, and the drawl that came out of her lover was...pure Texas. "Oh, darlin', you don't deserve that. You're a liar and a cheat."

"This is none of your business." Josie squeezed her hand. "I'm sorry. I shouldn't have lied to you, and I won't do it again. I love you, and I've learned my lesson. Come home with me, baby."

"No, Josie. No." She pulled her hand away.

"We have a good life there."

"Had. I have a better one now."

"What? With this tramp you just met?" Josie's eyes flashed. "What can she give you I can't?"

"Fidelity? Honesty? Respect? Honor?" Beks grinned at her, the expression fierce. "Shall I go on?"

"You're ridiculous. Marissa, this is a farce. You don't even know this woman. She's convenient. It's a rebound thing and you know it. Pack your bag, and let me take you home."

Beks leaned in and whispered soft, "Can we tell her *she* was the rebound?"

She laughed, and she didn't care if Josie thought it was at her. "I'm home. Go on, Josie. You'll be okay."

"We've got supper and a tarot reading before our naked whipped cream and cocoa plans tonight, so you'll have to excuse us." Beks stood up, with a smile that wouldn't melt butter.

"Gross." Josie tossed her head. "Fine. Goodbye, Marissa. Good luck with...this." Josie slid back into her black car and slammed the door.

She was going to need more time before all of this shit with Josie stopped confusing her and making her doubt herself, but she'd get over it.

She helped Beks with her crutches. "Do you think I need luck with this?"

"Nope. Luck offered us this. It's already in motion."

She watched Josie's car pull away. "I'm sorry. Again. At least I didn't cry this time." It was a close thing, though. She kind of wanted to.

"Oh, honey. Come on upstairs. We'll put our bags down and warm up, huh?" Beks gave her a gentle smile.

She stopped Beks before they got very far. "You're not a rebound, you know that right? I thought about that at first, but you're not. I'm done thinking short term and doubting this—doubting myself, doubting you."

Beks took her hand. "Thanks, Mari. I believe it, but it feels so good to hear it."

She smiled and helped Beks into the lobby. "Oh. Warm. I didn't realize how cold I was."

They headed up to what was their room for one more night. They dropped bags and backpacks, mitts and coats and hats in a messy heap before going to the sofa to slump down in a pile.

Bekka's cards were on the table waiting for them, and Mari wanted to see what was going to happen here, what Beks was going to tell her.

"You want me to read before we—"

The big French doors blew open, the winter wind blowing in and bringing snow.

"Oh my god." She hopped up, hurrying to the doors to close them, laughing. "Snow belongs outside."

"It does. It—man, my cards went fly—" Beks stopped and blinked.

"It's locked. I don't know how it just flew open like that. So weird." She watched Beks. "Are you okay?"

"Uh-huh." She picked the three cards up from the sofa. "Wow...look at this."

The first card was a lady who was lounging on a divan, with the Empress written on the bottom.

"That's a pretty one. She's...like, royalty?" She recognized some of the symbols for women on the card.

"Yes. I'm ready for love. That's what this one means, and this one?" A couple stood there, each holding a cup. "I love the way we communicate."

The final card she knew.

The Lovers.

She sat with Beks again. There wasn't any reason to be skeptical of that reading. "So this means we're perfect for each other, hm? I can totally believe in that."

"I—Yes. Yes, the universe seemed to be incredibly straightforward here, wouldn't you say?" Bekka stared at the cards with a wondering smile.

She wasn't going to think too hard about how the wind had actually drawn the cards, or that those doors had never blown open before. "Which one of these two people is me?" She chuckled, watching Beks.

"Funny girl. You're the angel, right? My fierce, wild angel?"

"Are you sure? Maybe you're mine, *darlin'*." She played with the word, mimicking that amazing drawl Beks had pulled from somewhere deep in those Texas roots to defend Marissa from her evil ex.

"Boobs to bones, honey. I'm in, no cheating, no bullshit, just you and me and making a life."

"And Poe. You and me and Poe." The no-bullshit part was maybe the best thing she'd heard in a long time. "I can't wait to move into our little house."

"I hope Poe likes me. I intend to make him a happy kitty." Beks lifted her face for a kiss. "Almost as happy as his mom."

"Good luck with that. I'm pretty damn happy." She gave Beks that kiss, lingering over it, letting it smooth out all her rough edges.

When she'd come out here, she'd been heartbroken, doing some guy she'd never met a favor, her world a wreck. Then a sweater-wrapped, tarot-reading whirlwind had slammed into her and demanded that she have some faith in the holidays.

It was like being bashed in the head with an elvish snow sprinkle.

Marissa hoped the magic never faded.

Never.

CHAPTER 14
ONE YEAR LATER

The Christmas lights reflected on the snow in the front yard, and the tree sparkled in the big window in the sitting room.

Thank goodness Lars had let them have a second one, after Poe had dragged the first one down and tried to haul all the ornaments in to the basement.

Bekka was fairly sure he was a demon in pretty kitty fur.

Marissa had laughed, like it was cute. It wasn't cute, because no cat should be able to do that. And yet there he was, looking innocent all curled up in Marissa's lap while she sat reading.

She couldn't believe that it had been a year. A year of moving and laughing, of buying the crazy little Victorian downtown that they'd rented after their fake honeymoon. A year of tarot readings and a little yoga practice three days a week. A year of kisses and laughing and making love on every surface of the house.

She looked up to find Marissa watching her. "I can hear you thinking from here. Are you nervous? What time does your booth open at the bazaar?"

"I'm going to have to leave in a few minutes. I'm not nervous, nervous, just—this is bigger than normal." And it was to raise money for the animal shelter.

Which was handy because the animal shelter had the new kitten they were going to pick up Monday.

"Oh. Geez." Marissa picked Poe up and sat him back down on the couch before hopping up. "I better get a sweater." Marissa kissed her cheek as she hurried by. "At least you're inside the barn where it's warmer."

"I know! And Lars says I can borrow Goober for my feet while she's giving sled rides."

"Goobie is a love," Marissa called from the bedroom. "He'll be the best foot warmer. Where is my red sweater? The heavy one?"

"In the laundry room, I think. You were line drying it." She headed to go grab it. "Can you get my cards and my tip jar?"

"Yeah, they're right here." Marissa came out of the bedroom with her things and they nearly walked right into each other. "Hi."

"Hey." She lifted her face for a kiss. "You ready to go be all festive together?"

"Mhm." Marissa kissed her, so easy and relaxed. "I'm off work until after Christmas." Mari traded her cards for the sweater and pulled it on. "Thank you. Cheerful right? Not that too many people will see it under my coat, but I'll feel Christmassy."

"You're perfect." Bekka put her hair up, making sure she mixed professional and mysterious perfectly. "Oh, did I mention our post-bazaar plans?"

Mari laughed. "No. But I'm not surprised you've made some."

"Well, the ladies have our karaoke playlist ready, and the tequila shots are on special tonight."

"Oh my god." Mari laughed. "Happy drunken karaoke-aversary!"

"No, love. *Merry* drunken karaoke-aversary to us."

Mari grabbed her, kissing her hard enough her lips burned. "Merry tram-orgasm, drunken karaoke-aversary, babe."

They had the best holiday memories. They got all bundled up in boots and coats and scarves and hats because Summit Springs was cold and snowy, and Mari grabbed the keys to their very used but snow-loving Subaru from the kitchen counter.

"You're going to rock this."

"You know it." Of course she would. She had her lover, she had a home, and they had a fun night ahead of them.

In fact, the ring burning a hole in her pocket sort of guaranteed it.

They were going to have a great holiday season, another wonderful year, and a Christmas wedding to plan.

Bekka had no doubt.

After all, it was fate.

THE END

Christmas Bizarre
Jodi Payne and BA Tortuga

Charlotte Miller is tired of feeling like a failure. She may have gotten herself fired, her love life has imploded...so when she gets the call that the annual Summit Springs Christmas Bazaar, which helps support her family's farm, is in trouble, she heads home to try to save the day. Maybe her luck will change and she will be happier for the holidays. Too bad her car decides to break down on the way.

Naomi "Lars" Beckett is too busy with the tree farm she runs and Christmastime to worry about a stranded hottie like Charlotte, but when they get snowed in together at an old cabin, she figures that's what she gets for trying to help. On the surface these two seem to have nothing in common, but opposites do attract, especially with the magic of the season, and they find they have more in common than they think. Once they're back in the crazy mix of family, well-meaning town folk, and trying to make things just right for Christmas though, will they be able to make something together that lasts longer than old wrapping paper and holiday leftovers?

Christmas Bizarre is a small town, opposites attract, lesbian romance set in fictional Summit Springs, Colorado.

Find it here!

I nterested in learning more about BA's cowboys and Jodi's gentlemen? Want free fiction and news? Join our newsletters!

What's Up with Jodi
https://readerlinks.com/l/2317334

Spurs and Shifters
https://lp.constantcontact.com/su/A9CRUzp/baandjulia

Happy Holidays, Y'all!

We want to thank you for giving Honeymoon in the Cards a try. We hope you enjoyed the story.

If you can spare a few minutes to post a review at the retail website where you made your purchase, we'd very much appreciate it!

Don't forget to "like" our Facebook pages and groups to keep up with all the news--new releases, sales announcements, giveaways, sneak peeks-- and of course the rodeo pictures, coffee memes and just general fun. We'd love to have all y'all!

Yeehaw and thanks for reading!

BA & Jodi

ABOUT JODI

JODI takes herself way too seriously and has been known to randomly break out in song. Her queer MCs are imperfect but genuine, stubborn but likable, often kinky, and frequently their own worst enemies. They are characters you can't help but fall in love with while they stumble along the path to their happily ever after. For those looking to get on her good side, Jodi's addictions include nonfat lattes, Malbec and tequila any way you pour it.

Website: jodipayne.net

Newsletter: https://readerlinks.com/l/2317334

All Jodi's Social Links: linktr.ee/jodipayne

ABOUT BA

Texan to the bone and an unrepentant Daddy's Girl, BA Tortuga spends her days with her basset hounds, getting tattooed, texting her grandbabies, and eating Mexican food. When she's not doing that, she's writing. She spends her days off watching rodeo, knitting and surfing Pinterest in the name of research. BA's personal saviors include her wife, Julia Talbot, her best friends, and coffee. Lots of coffee. Really good coffee.

Having written everything from fist-fighting rednecks to hard-core cowboys to werewolves, BA does her damnedest to tell the stories of her heart, which was raised in Northeast Texas, but has heard the call of the high desert and lives in the Sandias. With books ranging from hard-hitting GLBT romance, to fiery ménages, to the most traditional of love stories, BA refuses to be pigeon-holed by anyone but the voices in her head.

BA loves to talk to her readers and can be found at http://batortuga.com/ and her newsletter signup link is http://bit.ly/BAJulianews

AVAILABLE FROM JODI & BA

FF/Sapphic Romance

Christmas Bizarre, a Summit Springs Romance

Honeymoon in the Cards, a Summit Springs Romance

MM Romance

The Cowboy and the Dom Trilogy

First Rodeo, Book One

Razor's Edge, Book Two

No Ghosts, Book Three

The Soldier and the Angel, a Cowboy and Dom Novel

Sin Deep, a Cowboy and Dom Novel

Trouble with Cowboys - a Sin Deep Novel, coming January 2024!

East Meets Westerns

(single titles)

Wrecked

Flying Blind

Special Delivery, A Wrecked Holiday Novel

Temptation Ranch

Seeds and Sunshine

Pickup Man - Coming Spring 2024!

The Merry Everything Series

Cryptic